SOUL MUSIC: THE ILLUSTRATED SCREENPLAY

WYRD SISTERS: THE ILLUSTRATED SCREENPLAY

MORT – THE PLAY (adapted by Stephen Briggs)

WYRD SISTERS – THE PLAY (adapted by Stephen Briggs)

MEN AT ARMS – THE PLAY (adapted by Stephen Briggs)

GUARDS! GUARDS! – THE PLAY (adapted by Stephen Briggs)

MASKERADE (adapted for the stage by Stephen Briggs)❖

CARPE JUGULUM (adapted for the stage by Stephen Briggs)❖

LORDS AND LADIES (adapted for the stage by Irana Brown)❖

INTERESTING TIMES (adapted by Stephen Briggs)◆

THE FIFTH ELEPHANT (adapted by Stephen Briggs)◆

THE TRUTH (adapted by Stephen Briggs)◆

THE SCIENCE OF DISCWORLD (with Ian Stewart and Jack Cohen)❍

THE SCIENCE OF DISCWORLD II: THE GLOBE
(with Ian Stewart and Jack Cohen)❍

THE DISCWORLD COMPANION (with Stephen Briggs)¥

THE STREETS OF ANKH-MORPORK (with Stephen Briggs)

THE DISCWORLD MAPP (with Stephen Briggs)

A TOURIST GUIDE TO LANCRE – A DISCWORLD MAPP
(with Stephen Briggs and Paul Kidby)

DEATH'S DOMAIN (with Paul Kidby)

NANNY OGG'S COOKBOOK

THE PRATCHETT PORTFOLIO (with Paul Kidby)¥

THE LAST HERO (with Paul Kidby)¥

GOOD OMENS
(with Neil Gaiman)

STRATA

THE DARK SIDE OF THE SUN

THE UNADULTERATED CAT (illustrated by Gray Jolliffe)¥

* also available in audio   ¥ published by Victor Gollancz
❖ published by Samuel French   ◆ published by Methuen Drama
❍ published by Ebury Press   ✱ published by Oxford University Press

TERRY PRATCHETT

A JOHNNY MAXWELL story

JOHNNY
AND THE
DEAD

CORGI BOOKS

JOHNNY AND THE DEAD
A CORGI BOOK 0552 55412X

First published in Great Britain by Doubleday
an imprint of Random House Children's Books

Doubleday edition published 1993
Corgi edition published 1994
Reissued 2004

5 7 9 10 8 6

JF

Papers used by Random House Children's Books are natural,
recyclable products made from wood grown in sustainable forests.
The manufacturing processes conform to the environmental regulations
of the country of origin.

Set in 11.5/16pt Meridien by
Falcon Oast Graphic Art Ltd.

Corgi Books are published by Random House Children's Books,
61–63 Uxbridge Road, London W5 5SA,
a division of The Random House Group Ltd,
in Australia by Random House Australia (Pty) Ltd
20 Alfred Street, Milsons Point, Sydney, NSW 2061, Australia,
in New Zealand by Random House New Zealand Ltd,
18 Poland Road, Glenfield, Auckland 10, New Zealand
and in South Africa by Random House (Pty) Ltd,
Endulini, 5A Jubilee Road, Parktown 2193, South Africa

THE RANDOM HOUSE GROUP Limited Reg. No. 954009
www.kidsatrandomhouse.co.uk

A CIP catalogue record for this book is available from the British Library.

Printed and bound in Great Britain by
Cox & Wyman Ltd, Reading, Berkshire

Author's Note

I've bent history a little bit. There really were such things as Pals' Battalions, just as described here, and they really were a horribly innocent device for wiping out a whole generation of young men from one particular area with one cannon shell. But the practice died out by the summer of 1916, when the first Battle of the Somme took place. Nineteen thousand British soldiers died on the first day of the battle.

'Thomas Atkins' really *was* the name used on documents in the British Army in the way that people would now use 'A. N. Other', and 'Tommy Atkins' did become a nickname for the British soldier.

There were certainly a number of real Tommy Atkinses in the war. This book is dedicated to them – wherever they are.

Chapter 1

Johnny never knew for certain why he started seeing the dead.

The Alderman said it was probably because he was too lazy not to.

Most people's minds don't let them see things that might upset them, he said. The Alderman said he should know if anyone did, because he'd spent his whole life (1822–1906) not seeing things.

Wobbler Johnson, who was technically Johnny's best friend, said it was because he was mental.

But Yo-less, who read medical books, said it was probably because he couldn't focus his mind like normal people. Normal people just ignored almost everything that was going on around them, so that they could concentrate on important things like, well, getting up, going to the lavatory and getting on with their lives. Whereas Johnny just opened his eyes in the morning and the whole universe hit him in the face.

Wobbler said this sounded like 'mental' to him.

Whatever it was called, what it *meant* was this. Johnny saw things other people didn't.

Like the dead people hanging around in the cemetery.

The Alderman – at least, the *old* Alderman – was a bit snobby about most of the rest of the dead, even about Mr Vicenti, who had a huge black marble grave with angels and a photograph of Mr Vicenti (1897-1958) looking not at all dead behind a little window. The Alderman said Mr Vicenti had been a Capo de Monte in the Mafia. Mr Vicenti told Johnny that, on the contrary, he had spent his entire life being a wholesale novelty salesman, amateur escapologist and children's entertainer, which in a number of important respects was as exactly like not being in the Mafia as it was possible to get.

But all this was later. After he'd got to know the dead a lot better. After the raising of the ghost of the Ford Capri.

*

Johnny really discovered the cemetery after he'd
started living at Grandad's. This was Phase Three of
Trying Times, after the shouting, which had been
bad, and the Being Sensible About Things (which
had been worse; people are better at shouting).
Now his dad was getting a new job somewhere on
the other side of the country. There was a vague
feeling that it might all work out, now that people
had stopped trying to be sensible. On the whole,
he tried not to think about it.

He'd started using the path along the canal
instead of going home on the bus, and found
that if you climbed over the place where the wall
had fallen down, and then went around behind
the crematorium, you could cut off half the
journey.

The graves went right up to the canal's edge.

It was one of those old cemeteries you got owls
and foxes in and sometimes, in the Sunday papers,
people going on about Our Victorian Heritage,
although they didn't go on about this one because
it was the wrong kind of heritage, being too far
from London.

Wobbler said it was spooky and sometimes went
home the long way, but Johnny was disappointed
that it wasn't spookier. Once you sort of put out of

your mind what it *was* – once you forgot about all the skeletons underground, grinning away in the dark – it was quite friendly. Birds sang. All the traffic sounded a long way off. It was peaceful.

He'd had to check a few things, though. Some of the older graves had big stone boxes on top, and in the wilder parts these had cracked and even fallen open. He'd had a look inside, just in case.

It had been sort of disappointing to find nothing there.

And then there were the mausoleums. These were much bigger and had doors in, like little houses. They looked a bit like allotment sheds with extra angels. The angels were generally more life-like than you'd expect, especially one near the entrance who looked as though he'd just remem-bered that he should have gone to the toilet before he left heaven.

The two boys walked through the cemetery now, kicking up the drifts of fallen leaves.

'It's Halloween next week,' said Wobbler. 'I'm having a disco. You have to come as something horrible. Don't bother to find a disguise.'

'Thanks,' said Johnny.

'You notice how there's a lot more Halloween stuff in the shops these days?' said Wobbler.

'It's because of Bonfire Night,' said Johnny. 'Too many people were blowing themselves up with fireworks, so they invented Halloween, where you just wear masks and stuff.'

'Mrs Nugent says all that sort of thing is tampering with the occult,' said Wobbler. Mrs Nugent was the Johnsons' next door neighbour, and known to be unreasonable on subjects like Madonna played at full volume at 3 a.m.

'Probably it is,' said Johnny.

'She says witches are abroad on Halloween,' said Wobbler.

'What?' Johnny's forehead wrinkled. 'Like . . . Marjorca and places?'

'Suppose so,' said Wobbler.

'Makes . . . sense, I suppose. They probably get special out-of-season bargains, being old ladies,' said Johnny. 'My aunt can go anywhere on the buses for almost nothing and she's not even a witch.'

'Don't see why Mrs Nugent is worried, then,' said Wobbler. 'It ort to be a lot safer round here, with all the witches on holiday.'

They passed a very ornate mausoleum, which even had little stained-glass windows. It was hard to imagine who'd want to see in, but then, it was even harder to imagine who'd want to look out.

'Shouldn't like to be on the same plane as 'em,' said Wobbler, who'd been thinking hard. 'Just think, p'raps you can only afford to go on holiday in the autumn, and you get on the plane, and there's all these old witches going abroad.'

'Singing "Here we go, here we go, here we go"?' said Johnny.

'And "Viva a spanner"?'

'But I bet you'd get really *good* service in the hotel,' said Johnny.

'Yeah.'

'Funny, really,' said Johnny.

'What?'

'I saw a thing in a book once,' said Johnny, 'about these people in Mexico or somewhere, where they all go down to the cemetery for a big fiesta at Halloween every year. Like, they don't see why people should be left out of things just because they're dead.'

'Yuk. A picnic? In the actual cemetery?'

'Yes.'

'Reckon you'd get green glowing hands pushing up through the earth and nicking the sarnies?'

'Don't think so. Anyway ... they don't eat sarnies in Mexico. They eat tort ... something.'

'Tortoises.'

'Yeah?'

'I bet,' said Wobbler, looking around, 'I bet . . . I bet you wouldn't dare knock on one of those doors. I bet you'd hear dead people lurchin' about inside.'

'Why do they lurch?'

Wobbler thought about this.

'They always lurch,' he said. 'Dunno why. I've seen them in videos. And they can push their way through walls.'

'Why?' said Johnny.

'Why what?'

'Why push their way through walls? I mean . . . living people can't do that. Why should dead people do it?'

Wobbler's mother was very easy-going in the matter of videos. According to him, he was allowed to watch ones which even people aged a hundred had to watch with their parents.

'Don't know,' he said. 'They're usually very angry about something.'

'Being dead, you mean?'

'Probably,' said Wobbler. 'It can't be much of a life.'

Johnny thought about this that evening, after

15

meeting the Alderman. The only dead people he had known had been Mr Page, who'd died in hospital of something, and his great-grandmother, who'd been ninety-six and had just generally died. Neither of them had been particularly angry people. His great-grandmother had been a bit confused about things, but never angry. He'd visited her in Sunshine Acres, where she watched a lot of television and waited for the next meal to turn up. And Mr Page had walked around quietly, the only man in the street still at home in the middle of the day.

They didn't seem the sort of people who would get up after being dead just to dance with Michael Jackson. And the only thing his great-grandmother would have pushed her way through walls for would be a television that she could watch without having to fight fifteen other old ladies for the remote control.

It seemed to Johnny that a lot of people were getting things all wrong. He said this to Wobbler. Wobbler disagreed.

'It's prob'ly all different from a dead point of view,' he said.

Now they were walking along West Avenue. The cemetery was laid out like a town, with streets.

They weren't named very originally – North Drive
and South Walk joined West Avenue, for example,
at a little gravelled area with seats in. A kind of city
centre. But the silence of the big Victorian mausoleums made the place look as though it was
having the longest early-closing day in the world.

'My dad says this is all going to be built on,' said
Wobbler. 'He said the Council sold it to some big
company for fivepence because it was costing so
much to keep it going.'

'What, all of it?' said Johnny.

'That's what he said,' said Wobbler. Even he
looked a bit uncertain. 'He said it was a scandal.'

'Even the bit with the poplar trees?'

'All of it,' said Wobbler. 'It's going to be offices or
something.'

Johnny looked at the cemetery. It was the only
open space for miles.

'I'd have given them at least a pound,' he said.

'Yes, but you wouldn't have been able to build
things on it,' said Wobbler. 'That's the important
thing.'

'I wouldn't want to build anything on it. I'd have
given them a pound just to leave it as it is.'

'Yes,' said Wobbler, the voice of reason, 'but
people have got to work somewhere. We Need Jobs.'

'I bet the people here won't be very happy about it,' said Johnny. 'If they knew.'

'I think they get moved somewhere else,' said Wobbler. 'It's got to be something like that. Otherwise you'd never dare dig your garden.'

Johnny looked up at the nearest tomb. It was one of the ones that looked like a shed built of marble. Bronze lettering over the door said:

ALDERMAN THOMAS BOWLER
1822-1906
Pro Bono Publico

There was a stone carving of – presumably – the Alderman himself, looking seriously into the distance as if he, too, was wondering what Pro Bono Publico meant.

'I bet *he'd* be pretty angry,' said Johnny.

He hesitated for a moment, and then walked up the couple of broken steps to the metal door, and knocked on it. He never did know why he'd done that.

'Here, you mustn't!' hissed Wobbler. 'Supposing he comes lurchin' out! Anyway,' he said, lowering his voice a bit, 'it's wrong to try to talk to the dead. It can lead to satanic practices, it said on television.'

'Don't see why,' said Johnny.

He knocked again.

And the door opened.

Alderman Thomas Bowler blinked in the sunlight, and then glared at Johnny.

'Yes?' he said.

Johnny turned and ran for it.

Wobbler caught him up halfway along North Drive. Wobbler wasn't normally the athletic type, and his speed would have surprised quite a lot of people who knew him.

'What happened? What happened?' he panted.

'Didn't you see?' said Johnny.

'I didn't see anything!'

'The door opened!'

'It never!'

'It did!'

Wobbler slowed down.

'No, it didn't,' he muttered. 'No one of 'em can open. I've looked at 'em. They've all got padlocks on.'

'To keep people out or keep people in?' said Johnny.

A look of panic crossed Wobbler's face. Since he had a big face, this took some time. He started to run again.

'You're just trying to wind me up!' he yelled. 'I'm not going to hang around practising being satanic! I'm going home!'

He turned the corner into East Way and sprinted towards the main gate.

Johnny slowed down.

He thought: padlocks.

It was true, actually. He'd noticed it in the past.

All the mausoleums had locks on them, to stop vandals getting in.

And yet . . . and yet . . .

If he shut his eyes he could see Alderman Thomas Bowler. Not one of the lurchin' dead from out of Wobbler's videos, but a huge fat man in a fur-trimmed robe and a gold chain and a hat with corners on.

He stopped running and then, slowly, walked back the way he had come.

There was a padlock on the door of the Alderman's tomb. It had a rusty look.

It was the talking to Wobbler that did it, Johnny decided. It had given him silly ideas.

He knocked again, anyway.

'Yes?' said Alderman Thomas Bowler.

'Er . . . hah . . . sorry . . .'

'What do you want?'

'Are you *dead*?'

The Alderman raised his eyes to the bronze letters over the door.

'See what it says up there?' he said.

'Er . . .'

'Nineteen hundred and six, it says. It was a very good funeral, I understand. I didn't attend, myself.' The Alderman gave this some thought. 'Rather, I *did*, but not in any position where I could observe events. I believe the vicar gave a very moving sermon. What was it you were wanting?'

'Er . . .' Johnny looked around desperately. 'What . . . er . . . what does Pro Bono Publico *mean*?'

'For the Public Good,' said the Alderman.

'Oh. Well . . . thank you.' Johnny backed away 'Thank you very much.'

'Was that all?'

'Er . . . yes.'

The Alderman nodded sadly. 'I didn't think it'd be anything important,' he said. 'I haven't had a visitor since nineteen twenty-three. And then they'd got the name wrong. They weren't even relatives. And they were *American*. Oh, well. Goodbye, then.'

Johnny hesitated. I could turn around now, he thought, and go home.

And if I turn around, I'll never find out what happens next. I'll go away and I'll never know why it happened now and what would have happened next. I'll go away and grow up and get a job and get married and have children and become a grandad and retire and take up bowls and go into Sunshine Acres and watch daytime television until I die, and I'll never know.

And he thought: perhaps I did. Perhaps that all happened and then, just when I was dying, some kind of angel turned up and said would you like a wish? And I said, yes, I'd like to know what would have happened if I hadn't run away, and the angel said, OK, you can go back. And here I am, back again. I can't let myself down.

The world waited.

Johnny took a step forward.

'You're dead, right?' he said slowly.

'Oh, yes. It's one of those things one is pretty certain about.'

'You don't *look* dead. I mean, I thought . . . you know . . . coffins and things . . .'

'Oh, there's all that,' said the Alderman, airily, 'and then there's this, too.'

'You're a ghost?' Johnny was rather relieved. He could come to terms with a ghost.

'I should hope I've got more pride than that,' said the Alderman.

'My friend Wobbler'll be really *amazed* to meet you,' said Johnny. A thought crossed his mind. 'You're no good at dancing, are you?' he said.

'I used to be able to waltz quite well,' said the Alderman.

'I meant . . . sort of . . . like this,' said Johnny. He gave the best impression he could remember of Michael Jackson dancing. 'Sort of with your feet,' he said apologetically.

'That looks grand,' said Alderman Tom Bowler.

'Yes, and you have to have a glittery glove on one hand—'

'That's important, is it?'

'Yes, and you have to say "*Ow!*"'

'I should think anyone would, dancing like that,' said the Alderman.

'No, I mean like "Oooowwwwwwweeeeeah!", with . . .'

Johnny stopped. He realized that he was getting a bit carried away.

'But, look,' he said, stopping at the end of a

groove in the gravel. 'I don't see how you can be dead and walking and talking at the same time . . .'

'That's probably all because of relativity,' said the Alderman. He moonwalked stiffly across the path. 'Like this, was it? *Ouch!*'

'A bit,' said Johnny, kindly. 'Um. What do you mean about relativity?'

'Einstein explains all that quite well,' said the Alderman.

'What, *Albert* Einstein?' said Johnny.

'Who?'

'He was a famous scientist. He . . . invented the speed of light and things.'

'Did he? I meant Solomon Einstein. He was a famous taxidermist in Cable Street. Stuffing dead animals, you know. I think he invented some kind of machine for making glass eyes. Got knocked down by a motor car in nineteen thirty-two. But a very keen thinker, all the same.'

'I never knew that,' said Johnny. He looked around.

It was getting darker.

'I think I'd better be getting home,' he said; and began to back away.

'I think I'm getting the hang of this,' said the Alderman, moonwalking back across the path.

'I'll ... er ... I'll see you again. Perhaps,' said Johnny.

'Call any time you like,' said the Alderman, as Johnny walked away as quickly yet politely as possible. 'I'm always in.'

'Always in,' he added. 'That's something you learn to be good at, when you're dead. Er. Eeeeyooowh, was it?'

Chapter 2

Johnny raised the subject of the cemetery after tea.

'It's disgusting, what the Council are doing,' said his grandfather.

'But the cemetery costs a lot to keep up,' said his mother. 'No one visits most of the graves now, except old Mrs Tachyon, and she's barmy.'

'Not visiting graves has nothing to do with it, girl. Anyway, there's history in there.'

'Alderman Thomas Bowler,' said Johnny.

'Never heard of him. I was referring,' said his grandfather, 'to William Stickers. There was very nearly a monument to him. There *would* have been a monument to him. Everyone round here donated money, only someone ran off with it. And I'd given sixpence.'

'Was he famous?'

'Nearly famous. *Nearly* famous. You've heard of Karl Marx?'

'He invented communism, didn't he?' said Johnny.

'Right. Well, William Stickers didn't. But he'd have been Karl Marx if Karl Marx hadn't beaten him to it. Tell you what . . . tomorrow, I'll show you.'

It was tomorrow.

It was raining softly out of a dark grey sky.

Grandad and Johnny stood in front of a large gravestone which read:

WILLIAM STICKERS

1897-1949

WORKERS OF THE

WORLD UNIT

'A great man,' said Grandad. He had taken his cap off.

'What was the World Unit?' said Johnny.

'It should have been unite,' said Grandad. 'They ran out of money before they did the "E". It was a scandal. He was a hero of the working class. He would have fought in the Spanish Civil War except he got on the wrong boat and ended up in Hull.'

Johnny looked around.

'Um,' he said. 'What sort of a man was he?'

'A hero of the proletariat, like I said.'

'I mean, what did he look like?' said Johnny. 'Was he quite big with a huge black beard and gold-rimmed spectacles?'

'That's right. Seen pictures, have you?'

'No,' said Johnny. 'Not exactly.'

Grandad put his cap back on.

'I'm going down to the shops,' he said. 'Want to come?'

'No, thanks. Er . . . I'm going round to Wobbler's house.'

'Righto.'

Grandad wandered off towards the main gate.

Johnny took a deep breath.

'Hello,' he said.

'It *was* a scandal, them not giving me the "E",' said William Stickers.

He stopped leaning against his memorial.

'What's your name, comrade?'

'John Maxwell,' said Johnny.

'I knew you could see me,' said William Stickers. 'I could see you looking right at me while the old man was talking.'

'I could tell you were you,' said Johnny. 'You look . . . um . . . thinner.'

He wanted to say: not thin like in thick. Just . . . not all there. Transparent.

He *said*, 'Um.' And then he said, 'I don't understand this. You are dead, right? Some kind of . . . ghost?'

'Ghost?' said dead William Stickers angrily.

'Well . . . spirit, then.'

'There's no such thing. A relic of an outmoded belief system.'

'Um, only . . . you're talking to me . . .'

'It's a perfectly understandable scientific phenomenon,' said William Stickers. 'Never let superstition get in the way of rational thought, boy. It's time for Mankind to put old cultural shibboleths aside and step into the bright socialist dawn. What year is it?'

'Nineteen ninety-three,' said Johnny.

'Ah! And have the downtrodden masses risen up to overthrow the capitalist oppressors in the glorious name of communism?'

'Um. Sorry?' Johnny hesitated, and then a few vague memories slid into place. 'You mean like . . . Russia and stuff? When they shot the Tsar? There was something on television about that.'

'Oh, I know *that*. That was just the *start*. What's been happening since nineteen forty-nine? I expect the global revolution is well established, yes? No one tells us anything in here.'

'Well . . . there's been a lot of revolutions, I think,' said Johnny. 'All over the place . . .'

'Capital!'

'Um.' It occurred to Johnny that people doing quite a lot of the revolutions recently had said they were overthrowing communist oppressors, but William Stickers looked so eager he didn't quite know how to say this. 'Tell you what . . . can you read a newspaper if I bring you one?'

'Of course. But it's hard to turn the pages.'

'Um. Are there a lot of you in here?'

'Hah! Most of them don't bother. They just aren't prepared to make the effort.'

'Can you . . . you know . . . walk around? You could get into things for free.'

William Stickers looked slightly panicky.

'It's hard to go far,' he mumbled. 'It's not really allowed.'

'I read in a book once that ghosts can't move much,' said Johnny.

'Ghost? I'm just . . . dead.' He waved a transparent finger in the air. 'Hah! But they're not getting me *that* way,' he snapped. 'Just because it turns out that I'm still . . . here after I'm dead, doesn't mean I'm prepared to *believe* in the whole stupid nonsense, you know. Oh, no. Logical, rational thought, boy. And don't forget the newspaper.'

William Stickers faded away a bit at a time. The last thing to go was the finger, still demonstrating its total disbelief in life after death.

Johnny waited around a bit, but no other dead people seemed to be ready to make an appearance.

He felt he was being watched in some way that had nothing to do with eyes. It wasn't exactly creepy, but it *was* uncomfortable. You didn't dare scratch your bottom or pick your nose.

For the first time he really began to *notice* the cemetery. It had a leftover look, really.

Behind it there was the canal, which wasn't used any more, except as a rubbish dump; old prams and busted televisions and erupting settees lined its banks like monsters from the Garbage Age. Then on one side there was the crematorium and its Garden of Remembrance, which was all right in a gravel-pathed, keep-off-the-grass sort of way. In front was Cemetery Road, which had once had houses on the other side of it; now there was the back wall of the Bonanza Carpet (Save £££££!!) Warehouse. There was still an old phone box and a letter box, which suggested that once upon a time this had been a place that people thought of as home. But now it was just a road you cut through to get to the bypass from the industrial estate.

On the fourth side was nothing much except a wasteground of fallen brick and one tall chimney – all that remained of the Blackbury Rubber Boot Company. ('If It's a Boot, It's a Blackbury' had been one of the most famously *stupid* slogans in the world.)

Johnny vaguely remembered there'd been something in the papers. People had been protesting about something – but then, they always were. There was always so much news going on you never had time to find out anything important.

He walked round to the old factory site. Bulldozers were parked around it now, although they were all empty. There was a wire fence which had been broken down here and there despite the notices about Guard Dogs on Patrol. Perhaps the guard dogs had broken out.

And there was a big sign, showing the office building that was going to be built on the site. It was beautiful. There were fountains in front of it, and quite old trees carefully placed here and there, and neat people standing chatting outside it. And the sky above it was a glorious blue, which was pretty unusual for Blackbury, where most of the time the sky was that odd, soapy colour you'd get if you lived in a Tupperware box.

Johnny stared at it for some time, while the rain fell in the real world and the blue sky glittered on the sign.

It was pretty obvious that the building was going to take up more room than the site of the old boot factory.

The words above the picture said, 'An Exciting Development for United Amalagamated Consolidated Holdings: Forward to the Future!'

Johnny didn't feel very excited, but he did feel that 'Forward to the Future' was even dafter than 'If It's a Boot, It's a Blackbury'.

Before school next day he pinched the newspaper and tucked it out of sight behind William Stickers' grave.

He felt more daft than afraid. He wished he could talk to someone about it.

He didn't have anyone to talk to. But he did have three people to talk *with*.

There were various gangs and alliances in the

school, such as the sporty group, and the bright
kids, and the Computer Club Nerds.

And then there was Johnny, and Wobbler, and
Bigmac, who said he was the last of the well hard
skinheads but was actually a skinny kid with short
hair and flat feet and asthma who had difficulty
even *walking* in Doc Martens, and there was
Yo-less, who was technically black.

But at least they listened, during break, on
the bit of wall between the school kitchens and the
library. It was where they normally hung out – or
at least, hung around.

'Ghosts,' said Yo-less, when he'd finished.

'No-oo,' said Johnny uncertainly. 'They don't
like being called ghosts. It upsets them, for some
reason. They're just . . . dead. I suppose it's like not
calling people handicapped or backward.'

'Politically incorrect,' said Yo-less. 'I read about
that.'

'You mean they want to be called,' Wobbler
paused for thought, *'post-senior citizens.'*

'Breathily challenged,' said Yo-less.

'Vertically disadvantaged,' said Wobbler.

'What? You mean they're short?' said Yo-less.

'Buried,' said Wobbler.

'How about zombies?' said Bigmac.

'No, you've got to have a body to be a zombie,' said Yo-less. 'You're not really dead, you just get fed this secret voodoo mixture of fish and roots and you turn into a zombie.'

'Wow. What mixture?'

'I don't know. How should I know? Just some kind of fish and some kind of root.'

'I bet it's a real *adventure* going down the chippie in voodoo country,' said Wobbler.

'Well, you ought to know about voodoo,' said Bigmac.

'Why?' said Yo-less.

''Cos you're West Indian, right?'

'Do you know all about druids?'

'No.'

'There you are, then.'

'I 'spect your mum knows about it, though,' said Bigmac.

'Shouldn't think so. My mum spends more time in church than the Pope,' said Yo-less. 'My mum spends more time in church than *God*.'

'You're not taking this seriously,' said Johnny severely. 'I *really saw them*.'

'It might be something wrong with your eyes,' said Yo-less. 'Perhaps there's a—'

'I saw this old film once, about a man with X-ray

eyes,' said Bigmac. 'He could use 'em to see right through things.'

'Women's clothes and stuff?' enquired Wobbler.

'There wasn't much of that,' said Bigmac.

They discussed this waste of a useful talent.

'I don't see *through* anything,' said Johnny, eventually. 'I just see people who aren't ther— I mean, people other people don't see.'

'My uncle used to see things other people couldn't see,' said Wobbler. 'Especially on a Saturday night.'

'Don't be daft. I'm trying to be serious.'

'Yeah, but once you said you'd seen a Loch Ness Monster in your goldfish pond,' said Bigmac.

'All right, but—'

'Probably just a plesiosaur,' said Yo-less. 'Just some old dinosaur that ought to've been extinct seventy million years ago. Nothing special at all.'

'Yes, but—'

'And then there was the Lost City of the Incas,' said Wobbler.

'Well, I *found* it, didn't I?'

'Yes, but it wasn't that lost,' said Yo-less. 'Behind Tesco's isn't exactly lost.'

Bigmac sighed.

'You're all weird,' he said.

36

'All right,' said Johnny. 'You all come down there after school, right?'

'Well—' Wobbler began, and shifted uneasily.

'Not *scared*, are you?' said Johnny. He knew that was unfair, but he was annoyed. 'You ran away before,' he said, 'when the Alderman came out.'

'I never saw no Alderman,' said Wobbler. 'Anyway, I wasn't scared. I ran away to wind you up.'

'You certainly had me fooled,' said Johnny.

'Me? Scared? I watched *Night of the Killer Zombies* three times – with *freeze frame*,' said Wobbler.

'All right, then. You come. All three of you come. After school.'

'After *Cobbers*,' said Bigmac.

'Look, this is a lot more important than—'

'Yes, but tonight Janine is going to tell Mick that Doraleen took Ron's surfboard—'

Johnny hesitated.

'All right, then,' he said. 'After *Cobbers*.'

'And then I promised to help my brother load up his van,' said Bigmac. 'Well, not exactly promised . . . he said he'd rip my arms off if I didn't.'

'And I've got to do some geography homework,' said Yo-less.

'We haven't got any,' said Johnny.

'No, but I thought if I did an extra essay on rain-forests I could pull up my marks average,' said Yo-less.

There was nothing odd about this, if you were used to Yo-less. Yo-less wore school uniform. Except that it wasn't really school uniform. Well, all right, technically it was school uniform, because everyone got these bits of paper at the start of every year saying what the school uniform was, but no one ever wore it much, except for Yo-less, and so if hardly anyone else was wearing it, Wobbler said, how could it be a uniform? Whereas, said Wobbler, since at any one time nearly everyone was wearing jeans and a T-shirt, then really jeans and T-shirt *were* the *real* school uniform and Yo-less should be sent home for not wearing it.

'Tell you what,' said Johnny. 'Let's meet up later, then. Six o'clock. We can meet at Bigmac's place. That's right near the cemetery, anyway.'

'But it'll be getting dark,' said Wobbler.

'Well?' said Johnny. 'You're not scared, are you?'

'Me? Scared? Huh! *Me*? Scared? Me? *Scared?*'

If you had to be somewhere frightening when it got dark, Johnny thought, the Joshua N'Clement block rated a lot higher on the *Aaargh* scale than any cemetery. At least the dead didn't mug you.

It was originally going to be the Sir Alec Douglas-Home block, and then it became the Harold Wilson block, and then finally the new Council named it the Joshua Che N'Clement block after a famous freedom fighter, who then became president of his country, and who was now being an ex-freedom fighter and president somewhere in Switzerland while some of his countrymen tried to find him and ask him questions like: What happened to the two hundred million dollars we thought we had, and how come your wife owned seven hundred hats?

The block had been described in 1965 as 'an overwhelming and dynamic relationship of voids and solids, majestic in its uncompromising simplicity'.

Often the *Blackbury Guardian* had pictures of people complaining about the damp, or the cold, or the way the windows fell out in high winds (it was always windy around the block, even on a calm day everywhere else), or the way gangs roamed its dank passageways and pushed shopping trolleys off the roof into the Great Lost Shopping Trolley Graveyard. The lifts hadn't worked properly since 1966. They lurked in the basement, too scared to go anywhere else.

The passages and walkways ('an excitingly brutal brushed concrete finish') had two smells, depending on whether or not the Council's ninja caretaker had been round in his van. The other one was disinfectant.

No one liked the Joshua N'Clement block. There were two schools of thought about what should be done with it. The people who lived there thought everyone should be taken out and then the block should be blown up, and the people who lived *near* the block just wanted it blown up.

The odd thing was that although the block was cramped and fourteen storeys high, it had been built in the middle of a huge area of what was theoretically grass ('environmental open space'), but which was now the home of the Common Crisp Packet and Hardy-Perennial Burned-Out Car.

'Horrible place,' said Wobbler.

'People've got to live somewhere,' said Yo-less.

'Reckon the man who designed it lives here?' said Johnny.

'Shouldn't think so.'

'I'm not going too near Bigmac's brother,' said Wobbler. 'He's a nutter. He's got tattoos and everything. And everyone knows he pinches stuff. Videos and things. Out of factories. And he killed Bigmac's hamster when he was little. And he chucks his stuff out of the window when he's angry. And if Clint's been let out—'

Clint was Bigmac's brother's dog, which had reputedly been banned from the Rottweiler/Pit Bull Terrier Crossbreed Club for being too nasty.

'Poor old Bigmac,' said Johnny. 'No wonder he's always sending off for martial arts stuff.'

'I reckon he wants to join the Army so's he can bring his gun home one weekend,' said Yo-less.

Wobbler looked up apprehensively at the huge towering bulk of the block.

'Huh! Bringing his tank home'd be favourite,' he said.

Bigmac's brother's van was parked in what had been designed as the washing-drying area. Both the doors and the front wing were different colours. Clint was in the front seat, chained to the steering wheel. The van was the one vehicle that could be left unlocked anywhere near Joshua N'Clement.

'Weird, really,' said Johnny. 'When you think about it, I mean.'

'What is?' said Yo-less.

41

'Well, there's a huge cemetery for dead people, and all the living people are crammed up in that thing,' said Johnny. 'I mean, it sounds like someone got something wrong . . .'

Bigmac emerged from the block, carrying a stack of cardboard boxes. He nodded hopelessly at Johnny, and put the boxes in the back of the van.

'Yo, duds,' he said.

'Where's your brother?'

'He's upstairs. Come on, let's go.'

'Before he comes down, you mean,' said Wobbler.

'Shut up.'

The breeze moved in the poplar trees, and whispered around the antique urns and broken stones.

'I don't know as this is right,' said Wobbler, when the four of them had gathered by the gate.

'There's crosses all over the place,' said Yo-less.

'Yes, but I'm an atheist,' said Wobbler.

'Then you shouldn't believe in ghosts—'

'Post-living citizens,' Bigmac corrected him.

'Bigmac?' said Johnny.

'Yeah?'

'What're you holding behind your back?'

'Nothing.'

Wobbler craned to see.

'It's a bit of sharpened wood,' he reported. 'And a hammer.'

'*Bigmac!*'

'Well, you never know—'

'Leave them here!'

'Oh, all *right*.'

'Anyway, it's not stakes for ghosts. That's for vampires,' said Yo-less.

'Oh, *thank you*,' said Wobbler.

'Look, this is just the cemetery,' said Johnny. 'It's got by-laws and things! It's not Transylvania! There's just dead people here! That doesn't make it scary, does it? Dead people are people who were living once! You wouldn't be so daft if there were living people buried here, would you?'

They set off along North Drive.

It was amazing how sounds died away in the cemetery. There was only a set of overgrown iron railings and some unpruned trees between them and the road, but noises were suddenly cut right down, as if they were being heard through a blanket. Instead, silence seemed to pour in – pour *up*, Johnny thought – like breathable water. It hissed. In the cemetery, silence made a noise.

The gravel crunched underfoot. Some of the

more recent graves had a raised area in front of them which someone had thought would be a good idea to cover with little green stones. Now, tiny rockery plants were flourishing.

A crow cawed in one of the trees, unless it was a rook. It didn't really break the silence. It just underlined it.

'Peaceful, isn't it,' said Yo-less.

'Quiet as the grave,' said Bigmac. 'Hah, hah.'

'A lot of people come for walks here,' said Johnny. 'I mean, the park's miles away, and all there is there is *grass*. But this place has got tons of bushes and plants and trees and, and—'

'Environment,' said Yo-less.

'And probably some ecology as well,' said Johnny.

'Hey, look at this grave,' said Wobbler.

They looked. It had a huge raised archway made of carved black marble, and a lot of angels wound around it, and a Madonna, and a faded photograph in a little glass window under the name: Antonio Vicenti (1897–1958). It looked like a kind of Rolls Royce of a grave.

'Yeah. Dead impressive,' said Bigmac.

'Why bother with such a big stone arch?' said Yo-less.

'It's just showing off,' said Yo-less. 'There's probably a sticker on the back saying "My Other Grave Is A Porch".'

'*Yo-less!*' said Johnny.

'Actually, I think that was very funny,' said Mr Vicenti. 'He is a very funny boy.'

Johnny turned, very slowly.

There was a man in black clothes leaning on the grave. He had neat black hair, plastered down, and a carnation in his buttonhole and a slightly grey look, as if the light wasn't quite right.

'Oh,' said Johnny. 'Hello.'

'And what is the joke, exactly?' said Mr Vicenti, in a very solemn voice. He stood very politely with his hands clasped in front of him, like an old-fashioned shop assistant.

'Well, you can get these stickers for cars, you see, and they say "My Other Car is A Porsche",' said Johnny. 'It's not a very good joke,' he added quickly.

'A Porsche is a kind of car?' said dead Mr Vicenti.

'Yes. Sorry. I didn't think he should joke about things like that.'

'Back in the old country I used to do magical entertainment for kiddies,' said Mr Vicenti. 'With doves and similar items. On Saturdays. At parties. The Great Vicenti and Ethel. I like to laugh.'

'The old country?' said Johnny.

'The alive country.'

The three boys were watching Johnny carefully.

'You don't fool us,' said Wobbler. 'There's – there's no one there.'

'And I did escapology, too,' said Mr Vicenti, absent-mindedly pulling an egg from Yo-less's ear.

'You're just talking to the air,' said Yo-less.

'Escapology?' said Johnny. Here we go again, he thought. The dead always want to talk about themselves . . .

'What?' said Bigmac.

'Escaping from things.' Mr Vicenti cracked the egg. The ghost of a dove flew away, and vanished as it reached the trees. 'Sacks and chains and handcuffs and so on. Like the Great Houdini? Only in a semi-professional way, of course. My greatest trick involved getting out of a locked sack under-water while wearing twenty feet of chain and three pairs of handcuffs.'

'Gosh, how often did you do that?' said Johnny.

'Nearly once,' said Mr Vicenti.

'Come on,' said Wobbler. 'Joke over. No one's taken in. Come on. Time's getting on.'

'Shut up, this is interesting,' said Johnny.

He was aware of a rustling noise around him,

like someone walking very slowly through dead leaves.

'And you're John Maxwell,' said Mr Vicenti. 'The Alderman told us about you.'

'Us?'

The rustling grew louder.

Johnny turned.

'He's not joking,' said Yo-less. 'Look at his face!'

I mustn't be frightened, Johnny told himself.

I mustn't be frightened!

Why *should* I be frightened? These are just . . . post-life citizens. A few years ago they were just mowing lawns and putting up Christmas decorations and being grandparents and things. They're nothing to be frightened of.

The sun was well behind the poplar trees. There was a bit of mist on the ground.

And, walking slowly towards him, through its coils, were the dead.

Chapter 3

There was the Alderman, and William Stickers, and an old woman in a long dress and a hat covered in fruit, and some small children running on ahead, and dozens, *hundreds* of others. They didn't lurch. They didn't ooze any green. They just looked grey, and very slightly out of focus.

You notice things when you're terrified. Little details grow bigger.

He realized there were differences among the dead. Mr Vicenti had looked almost ... well, alive. William Stickers was slightly more colourless. The Alderman was definitely transparent around the edges. But many of the others, in Victorian clothes and odd assortments of coats and breeches from earlier ages, were almost completely without colour and almost without substance, so that they were little more than shaped air, but air that walked.

It wasn't that they had faded. It was just that they were further away, in some strange direction that had nothing much to do with the normal three.

Wobbler and the other two were still staring at him.

'Johnny? You all right?' said Wobbler.

Johnny remembered a piece about over population in a school geography book. For everyone who was alive today, it said, there were twenty historical people, all the way back to when people had only just *become* people.

Or, to put it another way, behind every living person were twenty dead ones.

Quite a lot of them were behind Wobbler. Johnny didn't feel it would be a good idea to point this out, though.

'It's gone all cold,' said Bigmac.

'We ought to be getting back,' said Wobbler, his voice shaking. 'I ought to be doing my homework.'

Which showed he *was* frightened. It'd take zombies to make Wobbler prefer to do homework.

'You can't see them, can you?' said Johnny. 'They're all around us, but you can't see them.'

'The living can't generally see the dead,' said Mr Vicenti. 'It's for their own good, I expect.'

The three boys had drawn closer together.

'Come on, stop mucking about,' said Bigmac.

'Huh,' said Wobbler. 'He's just trying to spook us. Huh. Like Dead Man's Hand at parties. Huh. Well, it's not working. I'm off home. Come on, you lot.'

He turned and walked a few steps.

'Hang on,' said Yo-less. 'There's something odd—'

He looked around at the empty cemetery. The rook had flown away, unless it was a crow.

'Something odd,' he mumbled.

'Look,' said Johnny. 'They're here! They're all around us!'

'I'll tell my mum of you!' said Wobbler. 'This is practising bein' satanic again!'

'John Maxwell!' boomed the Alderman. 'We must talk to you!'

'That's right!' shouted William Stickers. 'This is important!'

'What about?' said Johnny. He was balancing on his fear, and he felt oddly calm. The funny thing was, when you were on top of your fear you were a little bit taller.

'This!' said William Stickers, waving the newspaper.

Wobbler gasped. There was a rolled-up newspaper floating in the air.

'Poltergeist activity!' he said. He waved a shaking finger at Johnny. 'You get that around adolescents! I read something in a magazine! Saucepans flying through the air and stuff! His head'll spin round in a minute!'

'What is the fat boy talking about?' said the Alderman.

'And what is Dead Man's Hand?' said Mr Vicenti.

'There's probably a scientific explanation,' said Yo-less, as the newspaper fluttered through the air.

'What?' said Bigmac.

'I'm trying to think of one!'

'It's holding itself open!'

William Stickers opened the paper.

'It's probably just a freak wind!' said Yo-less, backing away.

'I can't feel any wind!'

'That's why it's freaky!'

'What are you going to do about this?' the Alderman demanded.

'Excuse me, but this Dead Man's Hand. What is it?'

'Will everyone SHUT UP?' said Johnny.

Even the dead obeyed.

'Right,' he said, settling down a bit. 'Um. Look, um, you lot, these . . . people . . . want to talk to us. Me, anyway—'

Yo-less, Wobbler and Bigmac were staring intently at the newspaper. It hung, motionless, more than a metre above the ground.

'Are they . . . the breath-impaired?' said Wobbler.

'Don't be daft! That sounds like asthma,' said Yo-less. 'Come on. If you mean it, say it. Come right out with it. Are they . . .' He looked around at the darkening landscape, and hesitated. 'Er . . . post-senior citizens?'

'Are they lurching?' said Wobbler. Now he and the other two were so close that they looked like one very wide person with six legs.

'You didn't tell us about this,' said the Alderman.

'This what?' said Johnny.

'In the newspaper. Well, it is *called* a newspaper. But it has pictures of women in the altogether! Which may well be seen by respectable married women and young children!'

William Stickers was, with great effort, holding the paper open at the Entertainment Section. Johnny craned to read it. There was a rather poor photo of a couple of girls at Blackbury Swimming Pool and Leisure Centre.

'They've got swimsuits on,' he said.

'Swimming suits? But I can see almost all of their legs!' the Alderman roared.

'Nothing wrong with that at all,' snapped the elderly woman in the huge fruity hat. 'Healthy bodies enjoying calisthenics in the God-given sunlight. And very practical clothing, I may say.'

'Practical, madam? I dread to think for what!'

Mr Vicenti leaned towards Johnny.

'The lady in the hat is Mrs Sylvia Liberty,' he whispered. 'Died nineteen fourteen. Tireless suffragette.'

'Suffragette?' said Johnny.

'Don't they teach you that sort of thing now? They campaigned for votes for women. They used to chain themselves to railings and chuck eggs at policemen and throw themselves under the Prince of Wales's horse on Derby days.'

'Wow.'

'But Mrs Liberty got the instructions wrong and threw herself under the Prince of Wales.'

'What?'

'Killed outright,' said Mr Vicenti. He clicked his disapproval. 'He was a very heavy man, I believe.'

'When you two have ceased this bourgeois argu-ing,' shouted William Stickers, 'perhaps we can get back to *important* matters?' He rustled the paper. Wobbler blinked.

'It says in this newspaper,' said William Stickers, 'that the cemetery is going to be closed. Going to be *built* on. Do you know about it?'

'Um. Yes. Yes. Um. Didn't *you* know?'

'Was anyone supposed to tell us?'

'What're they saying?' said Bigmac.

'They're annoyed about the cemetery being sold. There's a story in the paper.'

'Hurry up!' said William Stickers. 'I can't hold it much longer . . .'

The newspaper sagged. Then it fell through his hands and landed on the path.

'Not as alive as I was,' he said.

'Definitely a freak whirlwind,' said Yo-less. 'I've heard about them. Nothing supernat—'

'This is our *home*,' boomed the Alderman. 'What will happen to us, young man?'

'Just a minute,' said Johnny. 'Hold on. Yo-less?'

'Yes?'

'They want to know what happens to people in graveyards if they get built on.'

'The . . . dead want to know that?'

'Yes,' said the Alderman and Johnny at the same time.

'I bet Michael Jackson didn't do this,' said Bigmac. 'He—'

'I saw this film,' gabbled Wobbler, 'where these houses were built on an old graveyard and someone dug a swimming pool and all these skeletons came out and tried to strangle people—'

'Why?' said the Alderman.

'He wants to know why,' said Johnny.

'Search me,' said Wobbler.

'I think,' said Yo-less uncertainly, 'that the . . . coffins and that get dug up and put somewhere else. I think there's special places.'

'I'm not standing for that!' said dead Mrs Sylvia Liberty. 'I paid five pounds, seven shillings and sixpence for my plot! I remember the document Distinctly. Last Resting Place, it said. It didn't say After Eighty Years You'll Be Dug Up and Moved just so the living can build . . . what did it say?'

'Modern Purpose-Designed Offices,' said William Stickers. 'Whatever *they* are.'

'I think it means they were designed on purpose,' said Johnny.

'And how shameful to be sold for fivepence!' said dead Mrs Liberty.

'That's the living for you,' said William Stickers. 'No thought for the downtrodden masses.'

'Well, you see,' said Johnny wretchedly, 'the Council says it costs too much to keep up and the land was worth—'

'And what's this here about Blackbury Municipal Authority?' said the Alderman. 'What happened to Blackbury City Council?'

'I don't know,' said Johnny. 'I've never heard of it. Look, it's not *my* fault. I like this place, too. I was only saying to Wobbler, I didn't like what's happening.'

'So what are *you* going to do about it?' said the Alderman.

Johnny backed away, but came up against Mr Vicenti's Rolls-Royce of a grave.

'Oh, no,' he said. 'Not me. It's not up to me!'

'I don't see why not,' said dead Mrs Sylvia Liberty. 'After all, *you* can see and hear us.'

'No one else takes any notice,' said Mr Vicenti.

'We've been trying all day,' said the Alderman.

'People walking their dogs. Hah! They just hurry away,' said William Stickers.

'Not even old Mrs Tachyon,' said Mr Vicenti.

'And *she's* mad,' said the Alderman. 'Poor soul.'

'So there's only you,' said William Stickers. 'So

you must go and tell this Municipal whateveritis that we aren't . . . going . . . to . . . move!'

'They won't listen to me! I'm twelve! I can't even vote!'

'Yes, but we can,' said the Alderman.

'Can we?' said Mr Vicenti.

The dead clustered around him, like an American football team.

'We're still over twenty-one, aren't we? I mean, technically.'

'Yes, but we're dead,' said Mr Vicenti, in a reasonable tone of voice.

'You can vote at eighteen now,' said Johnny.

'No wonder people have no respect,' said the Alderman. 'I said the rot'd set in if they gave the vote to women—'

Mrs Liberty glared at him.

'Anyway, you can't use a dead person's vote,' said William Stickers. 'It's called Personation. I stood as Revolutionary Solidarity Fraternal Workers' Party Candidate. I know about this sort of thing.'

'I'm not proposing to let anyone use my vote,' said the Alderman. 'I want to use it myself. No law against that.'

'Good point.'

'I served this city faithfully for more than fifty years,' said the Alderman. 'I do not see why I should lose my vote just because I'm dead. Democracy. That's the point.'

'*People's* democracy,' said William Stickers.

The dead fell silent.

'Well . . .' said Johnny miserably. 'I'll see what I can do.'

'Good man,' said the Alderman. 'And we'd also like a paper delivered every day.'

'No, no,' Mr Vicenti shook his head. 'It's so hard to turn the pages.'

'Well, we must know what is happening,' said Mrs Liberty. 'There's no telling what the living are getting up to out there while our backs are turned.'

'I'll . . . think of something,' said Johnny. 'Something better than newspapers.'

'Right,' said William Stickers. 'And then you get along to these Council people and tell them—'

'Tell them we're not going to take this lying down!' shouted the Alderman.

'Yes, right,' said Johnny.

And the dead faded. Again there was the sensation of travelling, as if the dead people were going back into a different world . . .

'Have they gone?' said Wobbler.

'Not that they were here,' said Yo-less, the scientific thinker.

'They were here, and they've gone,' said Johnny.

'It definitely felt a bit weird,' said Bigmac. 'Very cold.'

'Let's get out of here,' said Johnny. 'I need to think. They want me to stop this place being built on.'

'How?'

Johnny led the way quickly towards the gates.

'Huh! They've left it up to me.'

'We'll help,' said Yo-less, promptly.

'Will we?' said Wobbler. 'I mean, Johnny's OK, but . . . I mean . . . it's meddlin' with the occult. And your mum'll go *spare*.'

'Yes, but if it's true then it's helping Christian souls,' said Yo-less. 'That's all right. They are Christian souls, aren't they?'

'I think there's a Jewish part of the cemetery,' said Johnny.

'That's all right. Jewish is the same as Christian,' said Bigmac.

'Not exactly,' said Yo-less, very carefully. 'But similar.'

'Yeah, but . . .' said Wobbler, awkwardly. 'I mean

. . . dead people and that . . . I mean . . . he can see 'em, so it's up to him . . . I mean . . .'

'We all supported Bigmac when he was in juvenile court, didn't we?' said Yo-less.

'You said he was going to get hung,' said Wobbler. 'And I spent all morning doing that "Free the Blackbury One" poster.'

'It was a political crime,' said Bigmac.

'You *stole* the Minister of Education's car when he was opening the school,' said Yo-less.

'It wasn't stealing. I meant to give it back,' said Bigmac.

'You *drove* it into a *wall*. You couldn't even give it back on a *shovel*.'

'Oh, so it was my fault the brakes were faulty? I could have got badly hurt, right? I notice no one worried about that. It was basically his fault, leaving cars around with Noddy locks and bad brakes—'

'I bet he doesn't have to repair his own brakes.'

'It's society's fault, then—'

'*Anyway*,' said Yo-less, 'we were behind you that time, right?'

'Wouldn't like to be in front of him,' said Wobbler.

'And we were right behind Wobbler when he

got into trouble for complaining to the record shop about the messages from God he heard when he played Cliff Richard records backwards—'

'You said you heard it too,' said Wobbler. 'Hey, you said you heard it!'

'Only after you told me what it was,' said Yo-less. 'Before you told me what I was listening for, it just sounded like someone going ayip-ayeep-mwerpayeep.'[1]

'They shouldn't do that sort of thing on records,' said Wobbler defensively. 'Gettin' at impressionable minds.'

'The point I'm making,' said Yo-less, 'is that you've got to help your friends, right?' He turned to Johnny. 'Now, *personally*, I think you're very nearly totally disturbed and suffering from psychosomatica and hearing voices and seeing delusions,' he said, 'and probably ought to be locked up in one of those white jackets with the stylish long sleeves. But that doesn't matter, 'cos we're friends.'

'I'm touched,' said Johnny.

'Probably,' said Wobbler, 'but we don't care, do we, guys?'

*

[1] But according to Wobbler it was *really*: 'Hey, kids! Go to school and get a good education! Listen to your parents! It's cool to go to church!'

His mother was out, at her second job. Grandad was watching *Video Whoopsy*.

'Grandad?'

'Yes?'

'How famous was William Stickers?'

'Very famous. Very famous man,' said the old man, without looking around.

'I can't find him in the encyclopedia.'

'Very famous man, was William Stickers. Haha! Look, the man's just fallen off his bicycle! Right into the bush!'

Johnny took down the volume L-MIN, and was silent for a few minutes. Grandad had a complete set of huge encyclopedias. No one really knew why. Somewhere in 1950 or something, Grandad had said to himself 'get educated', and had bought the massive books on hire purchase. He'd never opened them. He'd just built a bookcase for them. Grandad was superstitious about books. He thought that if you had enough of them around, education leaked out, like radioactivity.

'How about Mrs Sylvia Liberty?'

'Who's she?'

'She was a suffragette, I think. Votes for women and things.'

'Never heard of her.'

'She's not in here under "Liberty" or "Suffragette".'

'Never heard of her. Whoa, look here, the cat's fallen in the pond—!'

'All right . . . how about Mr Antonio Vicenti?'

'What? Old Tony Vicenti? What's he up to now?'

'Was he famous for anything?'

For a moment, Grandad's eyes left the TV screen and focused on the past instead.

'He ran a joke shop in Alma Street where the multi-storey car park is now. You could buy stink bombs and itchy-powder. And he used to do conjuring tricks at kids' parties when your mum was a girl.'

'Was he a famous man?'

'All the kids knew him. Only children's entertainer in these parts, see. They all knew his tricks. They used to shout out: "It's in your pocket!" And things like that. Alma Street. And Paradise Street, that was there, too. And Balaclava Terrace. That's where I was born. Number Twelve, Balaclava Terrace. All under the car park now. Oh, dear . . . he's going to fall off that building . . .'

'So he wasn't really *famous*. Not like *really* famous.'

'All the kids knew him. Prisoner of war in

Germany, he was. But he escaped. And he married
. . . Ethel Plover, that's right. Never had any kids.
Used to do conjuring tricks and escaping from
things. Always escaping from things, he was.'

'He wore a carnation pinned to his coat,' said
Johnny.

'That's right! Every day. Never saw him without
one. Always very smart, he was. He used to be a
conjuror. Haven't seen him around for years.'

'Grandad?'

'It's all changed around here now. I hardly see
anywhere I recognize when I go into town these
days. Someone told me they've pulled down the
old boot factory.'

'You know that little transistor radio?' said
Johnny.

'What little transistor radio?'

'The one you've got.'

'What about it?'

'You said it's too fiddly and not loud enough?'

'That's right.'

'Can I have it?'

'I thought you'd got one of those ghetto-
blowers.'

'This is . . . for some friends.' Johnny hesitated.
He was by nature an honest person, because apart

from anything else, lying was always too complicated.

'They're quite old,' he added. 'And a bit shut
in.'

'Oh, all right. You'll have to put some new batteries in – the old ones have gone all manky.'

'I've got some batteries.'

'You don't get proper wireless any more. We
used to get *oscillation* when I was a boy. You never
get it now. Hehe! There he goes – look, right
through the ice—!'

Johnny went down to the cemetery before break-
fast. The gates had been locked, but since there
were holes all along the walls this didn't make a lot
of difference.

He'd bought a plastic bag for the radio and had
sorted out some new batteries, after scraping out
the chemical porridge that was all that was left of
the old ones.

The cemetery was deserted. There wasn't a soul
there, living or dead. But there was the silence, the
big *empty* silence. If ears could make a noise, they'd
sound like that silence.

Johnny tried to fill it.

'Um,' he said. 'Anyone there?'

A fox leapt up from behind one of the stones and scurried away into the undergrowth.

'Hello? It's me?'

The absence of the dead was scarier than seeing them in the flesh – or at least, not in the flesh.

'I brought this radio. It's probably easier for you than newspapers. Um. I looked up radio in the encyclopedia and most of you ought to know what it is. Um. You twiddle the knobs and radio comes out. Um. So I'll just tuck it down behind Mr Vicenti's slab, all right? Then you can find out what's going on.'

He coughed.

'I . . . I did some thinking last night, and . . . and I thought maybe if people knew about all the . . . famous . . . people here, they'd be bound to leave it alone. I know it's not a very good idea,' he said, hopelessly, 'but it's the best I could come up with. I'm going to make a list of names. If you don't mind?'

He'd hoped Mr Vicenti would be about. He quite liked him. Perhaps it was because he hadn't been dead as long as the others. He seemed friendlier. Less stiff.

Johnny walked from gravestone to gravestone, noting down names. Some of the older stones were quite ornate, with fat cherubs on them. But one had a pair of football boots carved on it. He made a special note of the name:

STANLEY 'WRONG WAY' ROUNDWAY
1892-1936
The Last Whistle

He nearly missed the one under the trees. It had a flat stone in the grass, without even one of the ugly flower vases, and all it declared was that this was the last resting place of Eric Grimm (1885–1927). No 'Just Resting', no 'Deeply Missed', not even 'Died', although probably he had. Johnny wrote the name down, anyway.

Mr Grimm waited until after Johnny had gone before he emerged, and glared after him.

Chapter 4

It was later that morning.

There was a new library in the Civic Centre. It was so new it didn't even have librarians. It had Assistant Information Officers. And it had computers. Wobbler was banned from the computers because of an incident involving a library terminal, the telephone connection to the main computer, another telephone line to the computer at East Slate Air Base ten miles away, *another* telephone line to a much bigger computer under a mountain somewhere in America, and almost World War Three.

At least, that's what Wobbler said. The Assistant Information Officers said it was because he got chocolate in the keyboard.

But he was allowed to use the microfiche

readers. They couldn't think of a good reason to stop him.

'What're we looking for, anyway?' said Bigmac.

'Nearly everyone that died here used to get buried in that cemetery,' said Johnny. 'So if we can find someone famous who lived here, and then we can find them in the cemetery, then it's a famous place. There's a cemetery in London with Karl Marx in it. It's famous for him being dead in it.'

'Karl Marx?' said Bigmac. 'What was he famous for?'

'You're ignorant, you are,' said Wobbler. 'He was the one who played the harp.'

'No, Karl was the one who usedta talka lika dis,' said Yo-less.

'Actually, he was the one with the cigar,' said Wobbler.

'That's a very old joke,' said Johnny severely. 'The Marx Brothers. Hah, hah. Look, I've got the old newspaper files. The *Blackbury Guardian*. They go back nearly a hundred years. All we've got to do is look at the front pages. That's where famous people'd be.'

'And the back pages,' said Bigmac.

'Why the back pages?'

'Sports. Famous footballers and that.'

'Yeah, right. Hadn't thought of that. All right, then. Let's get started . . . '

'Yeah, but . . .' said Bigmac.

'What?' said Johnny.

'So this Karl Marx, then,' said Bigmac. 'What films was he in?'

Johnny sighed. 'Listen, he wasn't in any films. He was . . . he led the Russian Revolution.'

'No he didn't,' said Wobbler. 'He just wrote a book called, oh, something like *It's About Time There Was a Revolution*, and the Russians just followed the instructions. The actual leaders were a lot of people with names ending in *ski*.'

'Like Stalin,' said Yo-less.

'Right.'

'Stalin means Man Of Steel,' said Yo-less. 'I read where he didn't like his real name, so he changed it. It's Man of Steel in English.'

'What was his real name?'

'His secret identity, you mean,' said Yo-less.

'What are you talking about now?' said Bigmac.

'No, I get it. Man of Steel? Yo-less means he could leap Kremlins in a single bound,' said Johnny.

'Don't see why not,' said Wobbler. 'I always thought it was unfair, the way the Americans got

Superman. They've got all the superheroes. I don't see why we couldn't have had Superman round here.'

They thought about it. Wobbler then spoke for them all.

'Mind you,' he said, 'round here he would have had trouble even being Clark Kent.'

They disappeared under the hoods again.

'What did you say the Alderman was called?' said Wobbler, after a while.

'Alderman Thomas Bowler,' said Johnny. 'Why?'

'It says he got the Council to build a memorial horse trough in the square in nineteen hundred and five,' said Wobbler. 'It came in useful very quickly too, it says here.'

'Why?'

'Well . . . it says here, the next day the first motor car ever to arrive in Blackbury crashed into it and caught fire. They used the water to put the fire out. Says here the Council praised Alderman Bowler for his forward thinking.'

They looked at the microfilm viewer.

'What's a horse trough?' said Bigmac.

'It's that big stone trough thing that's outside Loggitt and Burnett's Building Society,' said

Johnny. 'The one that's been filled with soil for a tasteful display of dead flowers and lager cans. They used to put water in those things for coach horses to drink out of.'

'But if *cars* were just coming in,' said Bigmac slowly, 'then building things for horses to drink out of was a bit—'

'Yes,' said Johnny. 'I know. Come on. Let's keep going.'

... *WHEEEsssh* ... we built this city on ... *ssshshhh* ... on the phone right now ... *wheeesshhh* ... that was at Number Two ... *ssshwupwup* ... told a meeting in Kiev ... *wsswssshsss* ... Prime Minister ... *shsss* ... today ... *shhssss* ... scaramouche, can you ... *shssssss* ...

The tuning knob of the little radio behind Mr Vicenti's grave turned back and forth very slowly, as if it was being moved with great effort. Occasionally it would stop on a programme, and then move again.

... *ssshhhwwwss* ... and the next caller ... *shhwwsss* ... Babylon ...

And around it, for quite some distance, the air was cold.

*

In the library, the boys read on. Silence surrounded them. The Assistant Information Officers grew worried, and one of them went to find the cleaning fluid and the bent paperclip for getting chocolate out of keyboards.

'Let's face it,' said Wobbler, eventually, 'this is a town where famous people don't come from. It's famous for it.'

'It says here,' said Yo-less, from his viewer, 'that Addison Vincent Fletcher of Alma Terrace invented a form of telephone in nineteen twenty-two.'

'Oh, great,' said Wobbler. 'Telephones had been invented years before that.'

'It says he said this one was better.'

'Oh, yes,' said Wobbler. He dialled an imaginary number. 'Hello, is that— Who invented the real telephone, anyone?'

'Thomas Eddison,' said Yo-less.

'Sir Humphrey Telephone,' said Bigmac.

'Alexander Graham Bell,' said Johnny. 'Sir Humphrey *Telephone*?'

'Hello, Mr Bell,' said Wobbler, speaking into an imaginary mouthpiece, 'You know that telephone you invented years ago? Well, mine's better. And I'm just off to discover America. Yes, I know

Christopher Columbus discovered it first, but I'm discovering it *better*.'

'It makes sense,' said Bigmac. 'If you're going to discover somewhere, you might as well wait until there's proper hotels and stuff.'

'When did Columbus discover America, anyway?' said Wobbler.

'Fourteen ninety-two,' said Johnny. 'There's a rhyme: In fourteen hundred and ninety-two, Columbus sailed the ocean blue.'

Wobbler and Bigmac looked at him.

'Actually, he could have got there in fourteen ninety-one,' said Yo-less, without looking up, 'but he had to sail around a bit because no one could think up a rhyme for "one".'

'It *could* have been Sir Humphrey Telephone,' said Bigmac. 'Stuff gets named after inventors.'

'They didn't name the telephone after Bell,' said Wobbler.

'They named the *bell* after Bell, though,' said Bigmac. 'Telephone bells. Proves my point.'

'Telephones haven't had bells on for years,' said Wobbler.

'That,' said Yo-less, 'is due to the famous invention by Fred Buzzer.'

'I think it's *impossible* for anyone famous to come

from here,' said Wobbler, 'because everyone around here is mental.'

'Got one,' said Bigmac, turning the microfiche knob.

'Who? Which one?'

'The footballer. Stanley "Wrong Way" Roundway. He played for Blackbury Wanderers. There's his obituary here. Amost half a page.'

'Any good?'

'Says he scored a record number of goals.'

'Sounds good,' said Wobbler.

'Own goals.'

'What?'

'Greatest number of own goals in the history of any sport, it says. It says he kept getting over-excited and losing his sense of direction.'

'Oh.'

'But he was a good footballer, it says. Apart from that. Not exactly a Hall of Fame, though—'

'Here, look at this,' said Yo-less.

They clustered around his viewer. He'd found an ancient group photograph of about thirty soldiers, all beaming at the camera.

'Well?' said Wobbler.

'This is from nineteen sixteen,' said Yo-less. 'They're all going off to war.'

'Which one?' said Wobbler.

'The first one, you nerd. World War One.'

'I always wondered why they numbered it,' said Bigmac. 'Like they expected to have a few more. You know. Like Buy Two, Get One Free.'

'Says here,' Yo-less squinted, 'it's the Blackbury Old Pals Battalion. They're just going off to fight. They all joined up at the same time . . .'

Johnny stared. He could hear people's voices, and the background noises of the library. But the picture looked as if it was at the bottom of a dark, square tunnel. And he was falling down it.

Things outside the picture were inky and slow. The picture was the centre of the world.

Johnny looked at the grinning faces, the terrible haircuts, the jug-handle ears, the thumbs all up.

Even today nearly everyone in the *Blackbury Guardian* had their photo taken with their thumb up, unless they'd won Super Bingo, in which case they were shown doing what the photographer thought was a high kick. The newspaper's one photographer was known as Jeremy the Thumb.

The people in the picture didn't look much older than Bigmac. Well, a couple of them did. There was a sergeant with a moustache like a scrubbing brush, and an officer in jodhpurs, but the rest of them looked like a school photo.

And now he was coming back from wherever he'd been. The picture dropped away again, became just an oblong on a page on a screen. He blinked.

There was a feeling, like—

—like on an aeroplane when it's about to land, and his ears went 'pop'. But it was happening with his brain, instead.

'Anyone know what the Somme is?' said Yo-less.

'No.'

'That's where they went, anyway. Some place in France.'

'Any of them win any medals?' said Johnny, struggling back into the real world. 'That'd be famous. If there's someone in the cemetery with a lot of medals.'

Yo-less spun the wheels of the viewer.

'I'll look ahead a few issues,' he said. 'There's bound to be something if— Hey . . . look at *this* . . .'

They all tried to get under the hood at once. Silence came back as they realized what he'd found.

I knew it was important, Johnny thought. What's happening to me?

'Wow,' said Wobbler. 'I mean – all those names
. . . everyone killed in this big battle . . . '

Without saying anything, Johnny ducked into
the other reader and wound it backward until he
found the cheery photograph.

'Are they listed in alphabetical order?' he said.

'Yes,' said Yo-less.

'I'll read out the names under the photo, then.
Um . . . Armitage, K . . . Atkins, T . . .'

'Yes . . . no . . .' said Yo-less.

'Sergeant Atterbury, F . . .'

'Yes.'

'Hey, there's three from Canal Street,' said
Wobbler. 'That's where my gran lives!'

'Blazer . . . Constantine . . . Fraser . . .
Frobisher . . .'

'Yes . . . yes . . . yes . . . yes . . .'

They carried on to the end of the caption.

'They all died,' said Johnny, eventually.
'Four weeks after the picture was taken. All of
them.'

'Except for Atkins, T.,' said Yo-less. 'It says here
what a Pals' Battalion was. It says, people all from
one town or even one street could all join the
Army together if they wanted, and all get sent to
. . . the same place.'

'I wonder if they all got there?' said Yo-less. 'Eventually,' he added.

'That's dreadful,' said Bigmac.

'It probably sounded like a good idea at the time. Sort of . . . jolly.'

'Yes, but . . . four weeks . . .' said Bigmac. 'I mean . . .'

'You're always saying you can't wait to join the Army,' said Wobbler. '*You* said you were sorry the Gulf War was over. And all the legs of your bed are off the ground because of all them copies of *Guns and Ammo* underneath it.'

'Well . . . *yeah* . . . war, yeah,' said Bigmac. 'Proper fighting, with M16s and stuff. Not just all going off grinning and getting shot.'

'They all marched off together because they were friends, and got killed,' said Yo-less.

They stared at the little square of light with the names on it, and the long, long line of cheery thumbs.

'Except for Atkins, T.,' said Johnny. 'I wonder what happened to him?'

'It was nineteen sixteen,' said Yo-less. 'If he's still alive, he'll be dead.'

'Any of them on your list?' said Wobbler.

Johnny checked.

'No-oo,' he said, eventually. 'There's one or two people with the same name but the wrong initial. Everyone round here used to get buried up there.'

'Perhaps he came back from the war and moved away somewhere else,' said Yo-less.

'It'd be a bit lonely around here, after all,' said Bigmac.

They looked at him.

'Sorry,' he said.

'I'm fed up with this,' said Wobbler, pushing his chair back. 'It's not real. There's no one special in there. It's just people. And it's creepy. Come on, let's go down to the mall.'

'I've found out what happens to dead bodies when old graveyards are built on,' said Yo-less, as they stepped out into the Tupperware daylight. 'My mum knows. They get taken to some kind of storage place called a necropolis. That's Latin for City of the Dead.'

'Yuk,' said Wobbler.

'Sounds like where Superman lives,' said Bigmac. 'Necropolis!' said Wobbler, zooming his hands through the air. 'By day, mild-mannered corpse – by night . . . duh duh duhduh DAH . . . ZombieMan!'

JOHNNY AND THE DEAD

Johnny remembered the grinning young faces, not much older than Wobbler.

'Wobbler,' he said, 'If you make another joke like that—'

'What?'

'. . . well . . . just don't. Right? I mean it.'

. . . *ssshhhh* . . . mean, yo, youknowhatI'msayin'? . . . *sipsipsip* . . . told the government that . . . *sswwwsss* . . . fact the whales enjoy being hunted, Bob, and . . . *wwwhhhhh* . . .

Click!

'So that's wireless telegraphy, is it? Hah! So much for Countess Alice Radioni!'

'I was an Ovalteenie when I was a little boy. That was during the war. The one against the Germans. Did I ever tell you? We used to sing along with the people on the wireless: "We are the Ov—" WHAT? Who was Countess Alice Radioni?'

'Which war against the Germans?'

'What? How many have we had?'

'Two so far.'

'Now, come ON! Radioni? It was *Marconi* who invented the radio!'

'Hah! And do you know who he stole the idea from?'

'Who cares who invented the wretched thing? Will you listen to what the living are doing?'

'Plotting to steal our cemetery, that is what they are doing!'

'Yes, but . . . I didn't know that all this was going on, did you? All this music and . . . the things they were talking about! Who *is* Shakespeare's Sister and why is she singing on the wireless? What is a Batman? And they said the last Prime Minister was a woman! That can't be possible. Women can't even vote.'

'Yes, they can.'

'Hurrah!'

'Well, they couldn't in MY time!'

'There's so much we don't know!'

'So why don't we find out?'

The dead fell silent – or rather, more silent than usual.

'How?'

'The man on the wireless said you can ring the wireless station on the telephone to Discuss Problems That Affect Us All Today. A Phone-Ing Program, he said.'

'Well?'

'There's a phone box out in the street.'

'Yes, but . . . that's . . . outside . . .'

'Not far outside.'

'Yes, but . . .'

'The little boy stood in front of us and talked to us. And he was so frightened. And we can't walk six feet?'

The speaker was Mr Vicenti. He looked through the crumbling railings to the street outside, with the eye of a man who'd spent much of his life escaping.

'But this is our PLACE! This is where we BELONG!'

'It's only a few steps . . .'

It wasn't really much of a mall. But it was all there was to hang out in.

Johnny had seen films of American shopping malls. They must have different sorts of people in America, he'd thought. They all looked cool, all the girls were beautiful, and the place wasn't crowded with little kamikaze grandmothers. Or mothers with seven children. Or Blackbury United football fans walking ten abreast singing the famous football song, *'URRRurrrURRR-UH!'* (*clapclapclap*). You couldn't hang out properly in a place like that. All you could do was hang on.

The four of them hung on in the burger bar.

Yo-less carefully read the pamphlet about how no rainforests were chopped down to make beef-burgers. Bigmac had his favourite Megajumbo Fries with fifteen packets of relish.

'Wonder if I could get a job here?' said Wobbler.

'No chance,' said Bigmac. 'The manager'd take one look at you and see where the profits would go.'

'You saying I'm fat?' said Wobbler.

'Gravitationally challenged,' said Yo-less, without looking up.

'Enhanced,' said Bigmac.

Wobbler's lips moved as he tried these out. 'I'd rather be fat,' he said. 'Can I finish up your onion rings?'

'Anyway, there's loads of people want jobs here,' said Bigmac. 'You have to have three A-levels.'

'What, just to make burgers?'

'No other jobs around,' said Bigmac. 'They're shutting all the factories around here. Nothing to do. No one's making anything any more.'

'Someone's making something,' said Wobbler. 'What about all the stuff in the shops?'

'That's all made in Taiwanaland or somewhere. Hah! What sort of future are *we* going to have, eh? That's right, eh? Johnny?'

'What?'

'You've just been staring at nothing the whole time, you know that?'

'Yeah, what's happened?' said Wobbler. 'Some dead people come in for a takeaway?'

'No,' said Johnny.

'What're you thinking about, then?'

'Thumbs,' said Johnny, still staring at the wall.

'What?'

'What?' said Johnny, waking up.

'What about thumbs?'

'Oh . . . nothing.'

'My mother said last night that there's a lot of people angry about the cemetery being sold,' said Yo-less. 'Everyone's moaning about it. And Pastor William says anyone who builds on there will be cursed unto the seventh generation.'

'Yes, but he always says that kind of thing,' said Wobbler. 'Anyway, United Amalagamated Consolidated Holdings probably don't worry about that sort of thing. They've probably got a Vice-President in Charge of Being Cursed.'

'And he probably gets his secretary to deal with it,' said Bigmac.

'It won't stop anything, anyway,' said Yo-less. 'There's bulldozers just the other side of the fence.'

'Anyone know what United Amalagamated Consolidated Holdings *do*?' said Wobbler.

'It said in the paper that they're a multinational information-retrieval and enhancement facility,' said Yo-less. 'It said on the news it'll provide three hundred jobs.'

'For all the people who used to work at the old rubber boot factory?' said Bigmac.

Yo-less shrugged. 'That's how it goes,' he said. 'You all right, Johnny?'

'What?'

'You OK? You're staring at the wall.'

'What? Oh. Yeah. I'm OK.'

'He's upset about the dead soldiers,' said Wobbler.

Yo-less leaned across the table.

'Look . . . that's all in the past, right? It's just *gone*. It's a shame they died but . . . well . . . they'd be dead anyway, wouldn't they? It's just history. It's nothing to do with . . . well, with *now*.'

Mrs Ivy Witherslade was talking to her sister in the phone box on Cemetery Road when someone knocked impatiently on the glass, and that was odd, because there was no one there. But she felt very cold and suddenly uneasy, as though she was walking on someone's grave. She stopped telling her sister about her legs and what the doctor said about them, and went home quickly.

If Johnny had been there, he would have heard what happened next. But he wasn't, so everyone else would have just heard the wind, and perhaps, just perhaps, the faintest of arguments:

'You should know, Mr Fletcher. YOU invented it.'

'Actually, that was Alexander Graham Bell, Mrs Liberty. I just improved upon it.'

'Well . . . make it work. Let me speak to the man on the wireless machine.'

'Was it really Alexander Graham Bell?'

'Yes, Alderman.'

'I thought it was Sir Humphrey Telephone.'

The telephone stayed on its hook, but there were a few electric crackles and pops from somewhere in the machinery.

'I think I have mastered the intricacies, Mrs Liberty—'

'Let ME do the talking. The people's voice must be heard!'

Frost was forming on the inside of the telephone box.

'Certainly not. You are a bolshevik!'

'What did Sir Humphrey Telephone invent, then?'

'Mr Fletcher! Be so good as to expedite the electric communication!'

*

When there wasn't the burger bar to hang out in, and when they weren't allowed in J&J Software because of whatever Wobbler's latest crime was, there was only the fountain area with the sad, dying trees in it or Groovy Sounds record store, which was pretty much like any record store would be if it was called Groovy Sounds.

Anyway, Yo-less wanted to buy a tape for his collection.

'*Famous British Brass Bands*,' said Wobbler, looking over his shoulder.

'Yes, but this is a good one,' said Yo-less. 'It's got the old Blackbury Rubber Boot Factory Band playing *The Floral Dance*. Very famous piece.'

'You're just basically not black, are you,' said Wobbler. 'I'm going to report you to the Rastafarians.'

'*You* like reggae and blues,' said Yo-less.

'That's different.'

Johnny listlessly shuffled through the tapes.

And froze.

There was a voice he recognized. It was crackly with static, but it sounded a lot like Mrs Sylvia Liberty, and it was coming over the radio.

The radio was on the counter, tuned to

Wonderful Radio Blackbury's Mike Mikes Radio Show, which was as excellent and totally bodacious as two hours of phone-ins and traffic reports from the Blackbury bypass could be.

This time it was different. The phone-in had been about the Council's proposal to knock down the old Fish Market, which was going to happen no matter what anyone said, but it was a good subject for people to moan about.

'Well, what I say is *hello? Hello? This is Mrs Sylvia Liberty speaking on the electric telephone! Hello?* not to be allowed, er, in my opinion, er, it is totally *hello?* (click . . . fizz . . . crackle) *I demand to be heard this INSTANT! The Fish Market is of NO importance whatsoever!* er . . . er . . . and . . .'

In his little studio on top of the Blackbury and Slate Insurance Society, Mike Mikes stared at his engineer, who stared at his switchboard. There was no way of cutting off the intrusive voice. It was coming in on all telephone lines at once.

'Er, hi,' he said. 'The caller on . . . er . . . all the lines . . .'

'Here, someone's *You listen to me, young man! And don't cut me off to start playing any more of your phonograph cylinders!* crossed line here, Mike, I *Do you realize that innocent citizens are being EVICTED* (click

. . . garble . . . whirr . . . fizz) *many years of VALUED sevice to the community* (wheeeowwwwwh . . . crackle) *merely because of an ACCIDENT of birth* (fizzle . . . whipwhipwhip . . . crackle) *you listen to young Johnn* (snap . . . fizz . . .) *The People's Shroud is Deepest Black* (wheeeyooowwww . . . pop) *We're Coming BACK . . . stop that this minute, William, you are nothing but a bolshevik agit . . .'*

But no one heard the rest of the sentence because the engineer had pulled all the plugs and hit the switchboard with a hammer.

Johnny and his friends had gathered around the radio.

'You get some real loonies on these phone-ins,' said Wobbler. 'You ever listen to Mad Jim's Late Night Explosion?'

'He's not mad,' said Yo-less. 'He just says he is. And all he does is play old records and go "yeah!" and "yowsahyowsah!" a lot. That's not mad. That's just pathetic.'

'Yes,' said Wobbler.

'Yes,' said Bigmac.

'Yes,' said Yo-less.

They all looked at Johnny. They all looked like people with something on their minds.

'Ahem,' said Wobbler.

'Er,' said Bigmac.

'That was *them*, was it?' said Yo-less.

'Yes,' said Johnny. 'It was them.'

'It didn't sound like normal radio. How can they use the phone?'

'I don't know. I suppose some of them knew how to use the phone when they were alive. And maybe being dead's a bit like . . . electricity or something.'

'They nearly said your name,' said Wobbler.

'Yes.'

'Who was that one singing?'

'I think it was William Stickers. He's a bit of a communist.'

'I didn't think there were any communists left these days,' said Yo-less.

'There aren't. And he's one of them.'

'You know, any minute now Rod Serling is going to come walking in here with a big book,' said Bigmac. 'You know. Like in *The Twilight Zone*.'

'How come they know what's on the radio?' said Yo-less.

'I lent them Grandad's transistor.'

'You know what I think?' said Yo-less. 'I think you've started something.'

'That's what I think, too.'

'Nah!' said Wobbler. 'Come *on*! Voices on the radio? I mean! That's just mucking about. Could be anything. Kids ringing up and messing about. Oh, come *on*! Ghosts don't phone up radio stations!'

'I saw this film once where they came out of the telephone,' said Bigmac, winner of the All-Blackbury Mr Tactful Championship.

'Just you shut up! I don't believe you!'

It was very, very chilly inside the phone box.

'I must say, electricity is very easy to master when you're dead.'

'What are you doing, Mr Fletcher?'

'Very easy indeed. Who shall we talk to next?'

'We must speak to the Town Hall!'

'But it is a Saturday, Mrs Liberty. There will be no one there.'

'Then try to find young Johnny. I don't know what he means about trying to find famous people buried in the cemetery. WE'RE here, after all.'

'I'll keep trying. It's amazingly easy to understand.'

'Where's Mr Stickers gone?'

'He's trying to listen to Radio Moscow, whatever that is. On the wireless telegraphy apparatus.'

'I say, this is rather invigorating, you know. I've never been out of the cemetery before.'

'Yes. It's a new lease of life.'

'You can escape from almost anything,' said Mr Vicenti.

There was a faint cough. They looked around. Mr Grimm was watching them through the railings.

The dead seemed to sober up. They always became more serious in front of Mr Grimm.

They shuffled their spectral feet.

'You're outside,' said Mr Grimm. 'You know that's wrong.'

'Only a little way, Eric,' said the Alderman. 'That can't do any harm. It's for the good of the—'

'It's WRONG.'

'We don't have to listen to him,' said Mr Vicenti.

'You'll get into terrible trouble,' said Mr Grimm.

'No we won't,' said Mr Vicenti.

'It's dabbling with the Known,' said Mr Grimm. 'You'll get into dreadful trouble and it won't be my fault. You are bad people.'

He turned, and walked back to his grave.

'Dial the number,' said Mr Vicenti. The others seemed to wake up.

'You know,' said Mrs Liberty, 'he may have a point—'

'Forget about Mr Grimm,' said Mr Vicenti. He

opened his hands. A white dove shot out of his sleeve and perched on the phone box, blinking. 'Dial the number, Mr Fletcher.'

'Hello, directory enquiries, what name please?'

'He's called Johnny Maxwell and he lives in Blackbury.'

'I'm afraid that is not sufficient information—'

'That's all we—' (Listen, I can see how it works, there's a connection—)(How many of us are there in here?)(Can I try, please?)(This is a lot better than those seances) . . .

The operator rubbed her headset. For some reason, her ear had gone cold.

'Ow!'

She ripped it off.

The operator on her right leaned over.

'What's up, Dawn?'

'It went – it felt—'

They looked at the switchboard. Lights were coming on everywhere, and it was beginning to be covered in frost.

The point is—

—that all through history there have been people who couldn't invent things because the rest of the world wasn't ready. Leonardo da Vinci hadn't got the motors or materials to make his helicopter. Sir George Cayley invented the internal combustion engine before anyone else had invented petrol.[1]

And in his life Addison Vincent Fletcher had spent long hours with motors and relays and glowing valves and bits of wire, pursuing a dream the world didn't even have a name for yet.

In his phone box, dead Mr Fletcher laughed. It had a name now. He knew exactly what a computer was when he saw one.

[1]So he ran it on pellets of gunpowder. Really. It was nearly the *external* combustion engine.

Chapter 5

Johnny went home. He didn't dare go back to the cemetery.

It was Saturday evening. He'd forgotten about the Visit.

'You've got to come,' said his mother. 'You know she likes to see you.'

'No she doesn't,' said Johnny. 'She forgets who I am. She calls me Peter. I mean, that's my dad's name. And the place smells of old ladies. Anyway, why doesn't Grandad ever come? She's his wife.'

'He says he likes to remember her as she was,' said his mother. 'Besides, it's *Markie and Mo's Saturday Spectacular*. You know he doesn't like to miss it.'

'Oh . . . all right.'

'We don't have to stay long.'

*

About ten minutes after Johnny had gone, the phone rang. Grandad dealt with it in his normal way, which was to shout 'Phone!' while not taking his eyes off the screen. But it went on ringing. Eventually, grumbling and losing the remote control down the side of the cushion where it wouldn't be found for two days, he got up and shuffled out into the hall.

'Yes? He's not here. Gone out. Who? Well, I'll . . . is it? Never! Still doing the conjuring tricks, are you? Haven't seen you about the town much lately. No. Right. That's right. I don't get out much myself these days. How are you, in yourself? Dead. I see. But you've got out to use the telephone. It's wonderful, what they can do with science. You sound a long way off. Right. You are a long way off. I remember that trick you used to do with the handcuffs and the chains and – well, nearly did. Yes. Yes. Right. I'll tell him. Nice to hear from you. Goodbye.'

He went back and settled down in front of the TV again.

After a few minutes a small worried frown crossed his face. He got up and went and glared at the telephone for a while.

*

It wasn't that Sunshine Acres was a *bad* place. As far as Johnny could see, it was clean enough and the staff seemed OK. There were bright murals on the walls and a big tank of goldfish in the TV room.

But it was more gloomy than the cemetery. It was the way everyone shuffled around quietly, and sat waiting at the table for the next meal hours before it was due, because there wasn't anything else to do. It was as if life had stopped and being dead hadn't started, so all there was to do was hang around.

His grandmother spent a lot of time watching TV in the main lounge, or watching her begonias in her room. At least, his grandmother's body did.

He was never certain where her mind was, except that it was often far away and long ago.

After a while he got even more depressed at the conversation between his mother and his grand-mother, which was exactly the same as the one last week and the week before that, and did what he always did, which was wander out into the corridor.

He mooched towards the door that led out into the garden, staring vaguely at nothing.

They never told you about this ghost stuff at

school. Sometimes the world was so weird you didn't know where to start, and Social Education and GCSE Maths weren't a lot of help.

Why didn't this sort of thing happen to anyone else? It wasn't as if he went looking for it. He just tried to keep his head down, he just tried to be someone at the back of the crowd. But somehow everything was more complicated than it was for anyone else.

The thing was . . .

Mr T. Atkins.

He probably wouldn't have noticed it, except that the name was in the back of his mind.

It was written on a little curling piece of paper stuck in a frame on one of the doors.

He stared at it.

It filled the whole world, just for a second or two.

Well, there could be lots of Atkinses . . .

He'd never find out unless he knocked, though . . . would he? . . .

'Open the door, will you, love? M'hands are full.'

There was a large black woman behind him, her arms full of sheets. Johnny nodded mutely and turned the handle.

The room was more or less bare. There was certainly no one else there.

'I see you come up here every week to see your gran,' said the nurse, dumping the sheets on the bare bed. 'You're a good boy to come see her.'

'Uh. Yes.'

'What was it you were wanting?'

'Uh. I thought I'd . . . you know . . . drop in to have a chat with Mr Atkins? Uh.' Inspiration seized him. 'I'm doing a project at school. About the Blackbury Pals.'

A project! You could get away with anything if you said you were doing a project.

'Who were they then, dear?'

'Oh . . . some soldiers. Mr Atkins was one of them, I think. Uh . . . where . . . ?'

'Well, he passed away yesterday, dear. Nearly ninety-seven, I think he was. Did you know him?'

'Not . . . really.'

'He was here for *years*. He was a nice old man. He used to say that when he died the war'd be over. It was his joke. He used to show us his old Army pay book. "Tommy Atkins," he'd say. "I'm the one, I'm the boy, when I'm gone it's all over." He used to laugh about that.'

'What did he mean?'

'Don't know, dear. I just used to smile. You know how it is.'

The nurse smoothed out the new sheets and pulled a cardboard box from under the bed.

'This was his stuff,' she said. She gave him an odd look. 'I expect it's all right for you to see. No one ever visited him, except a man from the British Legion regular as clockwork every Christmas, God bless them. They've asked for his medals, you know. But I expect it's all right for you to have a look. If it's a project.'

Johnny peered into the box while the nurse bustled around the room.

There were a few odds and ends – a pipe, a tobacco tin, a huge old penknife. There was a scrapbook, full of sepia postcards of flowers and fields of cabbages and simpering French ladies dressed in what someone must once have thought was a very daring way. Yellowing newspaper cuttings were stuck between the pages. And there was a small wooden box lined with toilet paper and containing several medals.

And there was a photograph of the Blackbury Pals, just like the one in the old newspaper.

Johnny lifted it out very carefully, and turned it over. It crackled.

Someone had written, in violet ink, a long time ago, the words: *Old Comrades!!! We're the Boys, Kaiser Bill! If You Know A Better 'ole, Go To IT!!*

And there were thirty signatures underneath.

Beside twenty-nine of the signatures, in pencil, someone had made a small cross.

'They all signed it,' he said, quietly. 'He must have got a copy from the paper, and they all signed it.'

'What was that, dear?'

'This photo.'

'Oh, yes. He showed it to me once. That was him in the war, you know.'

Johnny turned it over again and found Atkins, T. He looked a bit like Bigmac, with jughandle ears and a second-hand haircut. He was grinning. They all were. All the same kind of grin.

'He used to talk about them a lot,' said the nurse.

'Yes.'

'His funeral's on Monday. At the crem. One of us always goes, you know. Well, you have to, don't you? It's only right.'

He dreamed, on Saturday night . . .

He dreamed of Rod Serling walking along Blackbury High Street, but as he was trying to speak impressively to the camera, Bigmac, Yo-less and Wobbler started to peer over his shoulder and say things like, 'What's this book about, then?' and 'Turn over the page, I've read this bit' . . .

He dreamed of thumbs . . .

And woke up, and stared at the ceiling. He still hadn't replaced the bits of cotton that held up the plastic model of the Space Shuttle. It was forever doing a nosedive.

He was pretty sure other kids didn't have lives like this. It just kept on happening. Just when he thought he'd got a grip on the world, and saw how it all worked, it sprang something new on him, and what he thought was the whole thing, ticking away nicely, turned out to be just some kind of joke.

His grandad had mumbled a very odd message when Johnny had arrived home. As far as he could understand, Wobbler or someone had been making odd phone calls. His grandad had also muttered something about conjuring tricks.

He looked at his clock radio. It said 2.45. There was no chance of going back to sleep. He tried Radio Blackbury.

'—yowsahyowsahyowsah! And the next caller on Uncle Mad Jim's bodaaaacious Problem Corner iiiissss—'

Johnny froze. He had a feeling . . .

'*William Stickers, Mad Jim.*'

'Hi, Bill. You sound a bit depressed, to *me*.'

'*It's worse than that. I'm dead, Jim.*'

'Wow! I can see that could be a real *downer*, Bill. Care to tell us about it?'

'*You sound very understanding, comrade. Well . . .*'

Of *course* he's understanding, thought Johnny as he struggled into his dressing gown. *Everyone* phones up Mad Jim in the middle of the night. Last week he talked for twenty minutes to a lady who thought she was a roll of wallpaper. *You* sound totally sane compared to most of them.

He snatched up his Walkman and switched on its radio so that he could go on listening as he ran down the stairs and out into the night.

'*—and now I just heard there isn't even ANY Soviet Union any more. What happened?*'

'Seems to me you haven't been keeping up with current events, Bill.'

'*I thought I explained about that.*'

'Oh, sure. You said. You've been dead. But you're alive again, right?' Mad Jim's voice had that little chuckle in it that it always got when he'd found a real dingdong on the line and could picture all his insomniac listeners turning up the volume.

'*No. Still dead. It's not something you get better from, Jim. Now*—'

Johnny pattered around the corner and sped along John Lennon Avenue.

Mad Jim was saying, in his special dealing-with-loonies velvet voice: 'So tell us all out here in the land of the living, Bill – what's it *like*, being dead?'

'*Like? LIKE? It is extremely DULL.*'

'I'm sure everyone out there would like to know, Bill . . . are there angels?'

Johnny groaned as he turned the corner into Eden Road.

'*Angels? Certainly not!*'

Johnny scurried past the silent houses and dodged between the bollards into Woodville Road.

'Oh, *dear*,' said Mad Jim in his headset. 'I hope there aren't any naughty men with pitchforks, then?'

'*What on earth are you blathering about, man? There's just me and old Tom Bowler and Sylvia Liberty and all the rest of them*—'

Johnny lost the thread of things when a sticking-out piece of laurel hedge knocked his headset off. When he managed to put it back on, it turned out that William Stickers had been invited to request a record.

'Don't think I know "The Red Flag", Bill. Who's it by?'

'*It's the Internationale! The song of the downtrodden masses!*'

'Doesn't fire a neuron, Bill. But for you and all the other dead people out there everywhere, tonight,' the change in Mad Jim's tone suggested that William Stickers had been cut off, 'and we're all dead sooner or later, ain't that the truth, here's one from the vaults by Michael Jackson . . . "Thriller"—'

The streetlamp by the phone box was alight.

And the little pool of light was all there was to see, unless you were Johnny . . .

The dead had spilled out on to the road. They'd managed to drag the radio with them. Quite a few of them were watching the Alderman.

'This is how you have to do it, apparently,' he said, moonwalking backwards across the frosty street. 'Johnny showed me.'

'It is certainly a very interesting syncopated rhythm,' said Mrs Liberty. 'Like this, you say?'

The ghostly wax cherries on her hat bounced up and down as she twirled.

'That's right. And apparently you spin around with your arms out and shout "*ow!*",' said the Alderman, demonstrating.

Oh no, thought Johnny, hurrying towards them. On top of everything else, Michael Jackson's going to *sue* me—'

'Get down and – what was it the man on the wireless said?' said the Alderman.

'Bogey, I believe.'

They weren't actually very good at it, but they made up for being eighty years behind the times by sheer enthusiasm.

In fact, it was a party.

Johnny stuck his hands on his hips.

'You shouldn't be doing this!'

'Why not?' said a dancing dead.

'It's the middle of the night!'

'Well? We don't sleep!'

'I mean, what would your . . . your descendants think if they could see you acting like this?'

'Serve them right for not visiting us!'

'We're making carpets!' shouted Mrs Liberty.

'Cutting a rung,' corrected one of the dead.

'A rug,' said the Alderman, slowing down a bit. 'A rug. Cutting a rug. That's what Mr Benbow who died in nineteen thirty-one, says it is called. Getting down and bogeying.'

'It's been like this all evening,' said Mr Vicenti. He was sitting on the pavement. In fact, he was sitting about half a metre *above* the pavement. 'We've found some very interesting stations. What exactly *is* a DJ?'

'A disc jockey,' said Johnny, giving up and sitting down. 'He plays the discs and stuff'

'Is it some kind of punishment?'

'Quite a lot of people like to do it.'

'How very strange. They are not mentally ill, or anything?'

The song finished. The dancers stopped twirling, but slowly and with great reluctance.

Mrs Liberty pushed her hat back. It had tipped over her eyes.

'That was extremely enjoyable,' she said. 'Mr Fletcher! Be so good as to instruct the man on the wireless to play something more!'

Interested despite himself, Johnny padded over to the phone box. Mr Fletcher was actually kneeling down with his hands *inside* the telephone. A couple of other dead people were watching him. One of them was William Stickers, who didn't look very happy. The other was an old man with a mass of white hair in that dandelion-clock style known as Mad Scientist Afro.

'Oh, it's you,' said William Stickers. 'Call this a world, do you?'

'Me?' said Johnny. 'I don't call it anything.'

'Was that man on the radio making *fun* of me, do you think?'

'Oh, no,' said Johnny, crossing his fingers.

'Mr Sticker iz annoyed because he telephoned Moscow,' said the white-haired man. 'They said they've had enough revolutions to be going on wiz, but vould like some soap.'

'They're nothing but dirty capitalists!' said William Stickers.

'But at least they want to be *clean* capitalists,' said Mr Fletcher. 'Where shall we try next?'

'Don't you have to put money in?' said Johnny.

Mr Fletcher laughed.

'I don't zink we've met,' said the white-haired man, extending a slightly transparent hand. 'Solomon Einstein (1861–1932).'

'Like Albert Einstein?' said Johnny.

'He vas my distant cousin,' said Solomon Einstein. 'Relatively speaking. Haha.'

Johnny got the impression Mr Einstein had said that line a million times, and still wasn't tired of it.

'Who're you ringing up?' said Johnny.

'We're just having a look at the world,' said Mr Fletcher. 'What are those things that go round and round in the sky?'

'I don't know. Frisbees?'

'Mr Vicenti just remembers them. They go round and round the world.'

'Oh. You mean satellites?'

'Whee!'

'But how do you know how to—'

'I can't explain. Things are a lot simpler, I think. I can see it all laid out.'

'All of what?'

'All the cables, all the . . . the satellites . . . Not having a body makes them a lot easier to use, too.'

'What do you mean?'

'For one thing, you don't have to stay in one place.'

'But I thought you—'

Mr Fletcher vanished. He reappeared a few seconds later.

'Amazing things,' he said. 'My word, but we shall have fun.'

'I don't underst—'

'Johnny?'

It was Mr Vicenti.

Someone living had managed to get through to Mad Jim. The dead, with much laughter, were trying to dance to a Country-and-Western number.

'What's going *on*?' said Johnny. 'You said you couldn't leave the cemetery!'

'No one has explained this to you? They do not teach you in schools?'

'Well, we don't get lessons in dealing with ghos— Sorry. Sorry. With dead people, I mean.'

'We're not ghosts, Johnny. A ghost is a very sad thing. Oh, dear. It's hard to explain things to the living. I was alive once, and I know what I'm talking about.'

Dead Mr Vicenti looked at Johnny's blank face. 'We're . . . something else,' he said. 'But now you see us and hear us, you're making us free. You're giving us what we don't have.'

'What's that?'

'I can't explain. But while you're thinking of us, we're free.'

'My head doesn't have to spin round and round, does it?'

'That sounds like a good trick. Can you make it do that?'

'No.'

'Then it won't.'

'Only I'm a bit worried I'm dabblin' with the occult.'

It seemed daft to say it, to Mr Vicenti in his

pinstripe trousers and little black tie and fresh ghostly carnation every day. Or Mrs Liberty. Or the big bearded shape of William Stickers, who would have been Karl Marx if Karl Marx hadn't been Karl Marx first.

'Dear me, I hope you're not dabbling with the occult,' said Mr Vicenti. 'Father Kearny (1891–1949) wouldn't like that at all.'

'Who's Father Kearny?'

'A few moments ago he was dancing with Mrs Liberty. Oh dear. We do mix things up, don't we?'

'Send him away.'

Johnny turned.

One of the dead was still in the cemetery. He was standing right up against the railings, clasping them like a prisoner might hold the bars of his cell. He didn't look a lot different to Mr Vicenti, except that he had a pair of glasses. It was amazing that they weren't melting; he had the strongest stare Johnny had ever seen. He seemed to be glaring at Johnny's left ear.

'Who's that?' he said.

'Mr Grimm,' said Mr Vicenti, without looking around.

'Oh, yes. I couldn't find anything about him in the paper.'

'I'm not surprised,' said Mr Vicenti, in a low and level voice. 'In those days, there were things they didn't put in.'

'You go away, boy. You're meddling with things you don't understand,' said Mr Grimm. 'You're imperilling your immortal soul. And theirs. You go away, you bad boy.'

Johnny stared. Then he looked back at the street, at the dancers, and the scientists around the telephone box. A bit further along there was Stanley Roundway, in shorts that came down to his knees, showing a group of somewhat older dead how to play football. He had 'L' and 'R' stencilled on his football boots.

Mr Vicenti was staring straight ahead.

'Um—' said Johnny.

'I can't help you there,' said Mr Vicenti. 'That sort of thing is up to you.'

He must have walked home. He didn't really remember. But he woke up in bed.

Johnny wondered what the dead did on Sundays. Blackbury on Sundays went through some sort of boredom barrier and out the other side.

Most people did what people traditionally do on Sundays, which was dress up neatly and get in the car and go for family worship at the MegasuperSaver Garden Centre, just outside the town. There was a kind of tide of potted plants that were brought back to get killed off by the central heating in time for next week's visit.

And the mall was locked up. There wasn't even anywhere to hang around.

'The point about being dead in this town,' said Wobbler, as they mooched along the towpath, 'is that it's probably hard to tell the difference.'

'Did anyone hear the radio last night?' said Johnny.

No one had. He felt a bit relieved.

'When I grow up,' said Wobbler, 'I'm going to be out of here like a shot. Just you watch. That's what this place is. It's a place to come from. It's not a place to stay.'

'Where're you going to go, then?' said Johnny.

'There's a huge big world out there!' said Wobbler. 'Mountains! America! Australia! Tons of places!'

'You told me the other day you'd probably get a job working at your uncle's place over on the trading estate,' said Bigmac.

'Yes . . . well . . . I mean, all those places'll be there, won't they, for when I get time to go,' said Wobbler.

'*I* thought you were going to be a big man in computers,' said Yo-less.

'I could be. I could be. If I *wanted*.'

'If there's a miracle and you pass Maths and English, you mean,' said Bigmac.

'I'm just more practically gifted,' said Wobbler.

'You mean you just press keys until something happens.'

'Well? Often things *do* happen.'

'*I'm* going to join the Army,' said Bigmac. 'The SAS.'

'Huh. The flat feet and the asthma will be a big help there, then,' said Wobbler. 'I can just see they'll want you to limp out and wheeze on terrorists.'

'I'm pretty certain I want to get a law degree and a medical degree,' said Yo-less, to keep the peace.

'That's good. That way they won't be able to sue you if you chop the wrong bits off,' said Bigmac.

No one really lost their temper. This was all part of hanging around.

'What about you?' said Wobbler. 'What do you want to be?'

'Dunno,' said Johnny.

'Didn't you go to the careers evening last week?'

Johnny nodded. It had been full of Great Futures.

There was a Great Future in retail marketing. There was a Great Future in wholesale distribution. There was a Great Future in the armed forces, although probably not for Bigmac, who'd been allowed to hold a machine gun and had dropped it on his foot. But Johnny couldn't find a Great Future with any future in it.

'What I want to be,' he said, 'is something they haven't got a name for yet.'

'Oh, yeah?' said Wobbler. 'Like, in two years time someone's going to invent the Vurglesplat, and when they start looking around for Vurglesplat operators, you're going to be first in the queue, right?'

They went through the cemetery. The others, without saying anything, bunched up slightly. But there were no dead people around.

'You can't just hang around waiting for Great Futures, that's the point,' Johnny murmured.

'Hey,' said Yo-less, in a dismally jolly voice, 'my mum says why don't you guys come to church tonight?'

'It won't work,' said Wobbler, after a while. 'You say that every week.'

'She says it'd be good for you. Especially Simon.'

'Simon?' said Wobbler.

'Me,' said Bigmac.

'She says you need looking after,' said Yo-less.

'I didn't know you were called Simon,' said Wobbler.

Bigmac sighed. He had 'Blackbury Skins' on his T-shirt, a suede haircut, great big boots, great big braces and LOVE and HAT in Biro on his knuckles[1], but for some reason Yo-less's mum thought he needed a proper home. Bigmac lived in dread that Bazza and Skazz, the only other Skins in Blackbury, would find out and confiscate his official braces.

'She said you're all growing up heathens,' said Yo-less.

'Well, I'm going to a funeral at the crem tomorrow,' said Johnny. 'That's almost church.'

'Anyone important?' said Wobbler.

'I'm not sure,' said Johnny.

Johnny was amazed that so many people had come to Thomas Atkins's funeral, but that was because they'd really come to the one before it. All there was for Atkins's was himself and a stiff-looking old man in a blazer from the British Legion

[1]The 'E' kept rubbing off.

and the nurse from Sunshine Acres. And the vicar, who did his best, but had never met Tommy Atkins so had to put together his sermon out of a sort of kit of Proper Things to Say. And then some recorded organ music. And that was it.

The chapel smelled of new wood and floor polish.

The three others kept looking at Johnny in an embarrassed way, as if they felt he shouldn't be there but didn't know exactly how to put it.

He heard a faint sound behind him, just as the recorded music started up.

He turned around, and there were the dead, seated in rows. The Alderman had taken his hat off and was sitting stiffly at attention. Even William Stickers had tried to look respectable. Solomon Einstein's hair stood out like a halo.

The nurse was talking to the man in the blazer. Johnny leaned back so that he could speak to Mr Fletcher.

'Why are you here?' he whispered.

'It's allowed,' said Mr Fletcher. 'We used to go to all the funerals in the cemetery. Help them settle in. Make them welcome. It's always a bit of a shock.'

'Oh.'

'And . . . seeing as you were here . . . we thought we'd see if we could make it. Mr Vicenti said it was worth a try. We're getting better at it!'

The nurse handed Tommy Atkins's box to the British Legion man and walked out, waving at Johnny uncertainly as she went past. And then the vicar ushered the man through another door, giving Johnny another funny look.

Outside, the October sun was shining weakly, but it was managing to shine. Johnny went outside and waited.

Eventually the man came out, holding two boxes this time.

'Uh,' said Johnny, standing up. 'Um.'

'Yes, lad? The lady from the Home said you're doing a project for school.'

Doing a project. It was amazing. If Saddam Hussein had said he was doing a school project on Kuwait, he'd have found life a lot easier . . .

'Um, yes. Uh. Can I ask you some stuff?'

'Of course, yes.' The man sat down heavily on one of the benches. He walked with a limp, and sat with one leg stretched out straight in front of him. Johnny was surprised to see that he was probably as old as Grandad, but he had that dried-out, sun-tanned look of a man who keeps himself fit and is probably still going to be captain of the bowls club when he's eighty.

'Well . . . when Mr Atkins said . . .' Johnny began. 'I mean, he used to say that he was "the one". I know about the Blackbury Pals. I know they all got killed except him. But I don't think that's what he meant . . .'

'You know about the Pals, do you? How?'

'Read it in an old newspaper.'

'Oh. But you don't know about Tommy Atkins?'

'Well, yes, he—'

'No, I mean *Tommy Atkins*. I meant, why he was so proud of the name. What the name *meant*?'

'I don't understand that,' said Johnny.

'What do they teach you in school these days?'

Johnny didn't answer. He could tell it wasn't really a question.

'You see – in the Great War, the First World War . . . when a new recruit joined the Army he had to fill in his pay book, yes? You know? Name and address and that sort of thing? And to help them do it, the Army did a kind of guide to how to fill it in, and on the guide, where it said Name, they put: Thomas Atkins. It was just a name. Just to show them that's where their name should be. Like: John Smith. But it . . . well, it became a sort of joke. Tommy Atkins came to mean the average soldier—'

'Like The Man In The Street?'

'Yes . . . very much like that. It was a nickname for a soldier, I do know that. Tommy Atkins – the British Tommy.'

'So . . . in a way . . . *all* soldiers were Tommy Atkins?'

'Yes. I suppose you could put it like that. Of course, that's a rather fanciful way of—'

'But he was a real person. He smoked a pipe and everything.'

'Well, I suppose the Army used it because they thought it was a common sort of name. So there was bound to be a *real* Tommy Atkins somewhere. I know he was very proud of his name. I do know that.'

'Was he the last man alive who fought in the war?'

'Oh, no. Good heavens, no. But he was the last one from around here, that's for certain. The last of the Pals.'

Johnny felt a change in the air.

'He was a strange old boy. I used to go and see him every year at—'

There was a noise that might be made if a handful

of silence was stretched thin and then plucked, like a guitar string.

Johnny looked around. Now there were three people sitting on the bench.

Tommy Atkins had his peaked hat on his knees. The uniform didn't really fit. He was still an old man, so his skinny neck stuck out of his collar like a tortoise's. He had an old-fashioned sort of face – one designed to wear a cloth cap and work in the rubber boot factory. He saw Johnny staring at him, and winked, and gave him the thumbs-up sign. Then he went back to gazing intently at the road leading into the car park.

Behind Johnny, the dead filed quietly out of the building, the older ones coming through the wall, the younger ones still using the door out of habit. They didn't say anything. They just stood and looked expectantly towards the main road.

Where, marching *through* the cars, were the Blackbury Pals.

Chapter 6

The Pals swung up the road, keeping perfectly in step.

None of them were old. They all looked like their photograph.

But then, Tommy Atkins didn't look old any more. It was a young man who got to his feet, marched out into the car park, turned, and saluted Johnny and the dead.

Then, as the Pals strode past, he stepped neatly into the gap they'd left for him. All thirty men wheeled about, and marched away.

The dead streamed after them. They appeared to walk slowly while at the same time moved very fast, so that, in a few seconds, the car park was empty even of its ghosts.

'He's going back to France,' said Johnny.

Suddenly, he felt quite cheerful, even though he could feel the tears running down his face.

The British Legion man, who had been talking, stopped.

'What?' he said.

'Tommy Atkins. He's going back.'

'How did you know that?'

Johnny realized he'd been talking aloud.

'Uh—'

The British Legion man relaxed.

'I expect the lady from the Home told you, did she? He mentioned it in his will. Would you like a handkerchief?'

'Uh. No. I'm all right,' said Johnny. 'Yes. She told me.'

'Yes, we're taking him back this week. He gave us a map reference. Very precise, too.' The man patted the second box he'd been given which, Johnny suddenly realized, probably contained all that was left in this world of Atkins, T., apart from a few medals and some faded photographs.

'What will you have to do?' he said.

'Just scatter his ashes. We'll have a little ceremony.'

'Where . . . the Pals died?'

'That's right. He was always talking about them, I do know that.'

'Sir?'

The man looked up.

'Yes?'

'My name's John Maxwell. What's yours?'

'Atterbury. Ronald Atterbury.'

He extended a hand. They shook hands, solemnly.

'Are you Arthur Maxwell's grandson? He used to work for me at the boot factory.'

'Yes. Sir?'

'Yes?'

Johnny knew what the answer was going to be. He could feel it looming ahead of him. But you had to ask the question, so that the answer could exist. He took a deep breath.

'Are you related to Sergeant Atterbury? He was one of the Pals.'

'He was my father.'

'Oh.'

'I never saw him. He married my mother before he went off to the war. There was a lot of that sort of thing. There always is. Excuse me, young man, but shouldn't you be in school?'

'No,' said Johnny.

'Really?'

'I should be here. I'm absolutely sure about that,' said Johnny. 'But I'd better be getting to school, anyway. Thanks for talking to me.'

'I hope you haven't missed any important lessons.'

'History.'

'That's very important.'

'Can I ask you one more question?'

'Yes?'

'Tommy Atkins's medals. Were they for anything special?'

'They were campaign medals. Soldiers got them, really, for just staying alive. And for being there. He went all the way through the war, you know. Right to the end. Didn't even get wounded.'

Johnny walked back down the drive barely noticing the world around him. Something important had happened, and he alone of all the living had seen it, and it was *right*.

Getting medals for being there was right, too. Sometimes being there was all you could do.

He looked back when he reached the road. Mr Atterbury was still sitting on the bench with the two boxes beside him, staring at the trees as if he'd never seen them before. Just staring, as if he

JOHNNY AND THE DEAD

could see right through them, all the way to France.

Johnny hesitated, and then started back.

'No,' said Mr Vicenti, right behind him.

He'd been waiting by the bus shelter. Haunting it, almost.

'I was only going to—'

'Yes, you were,' said Mr Vicenti. 'And what would you say? That you'd seen them? What good would that do? Perhaps he's seeing them too, inside his head.'

'Well—'

'It wouldn't work.'

'But if I—'

'If you did something like that a few hundred years ago you'd probably be hung for witchcraft. Last century they'd lock you up. I don't know what they'd do now.'

Johnny relaxed a little. The urge to run back up the driveway had faded.

'Put me on television, I expect,' he said, walking along the road.

'Well, we don't want that,' said Mr Vicenti. He walked too, although his feet didn't always meet the ground.

'It's just that if I could make people see that—'

127

'Maybe,' said Mr Vicenti. 'But making people see anything is a long, hard job – excuse me . . .'

He jerked his shoulder a bit, like a man trying to find a difficult itch, and then pulled a pair of doves from inside his jacket.

'They breed in there, I'm sure,' he said, watching them fly away and disappear. 'What are you going to do now?'

'School. And don't say it's very important.'

'I said nothing.'

They reached the entrance to the cemetery. Johnny could just see the big sign on the old factory site next door, its blue sky glowing against the dustier blue-grey of the real sky.

'They'll start taking us out the day after tomorrow,' said Mr Vicenti.

'I'm sorry. Like I said, I wish there was something I could do.'

'You may have done it already.'

Johnny sighed.

'If I ask you what you mean, you'll say it's hard to explain, right?'

'I think so. Come. You might enjoy this.'

There wasn't even a dead soul in the cemetery. Even the rook had gone, unless it was a crow.

But there was a lot of noise coming from the canal.

*

The dead were swimming. Well, some of them were. Mrs Liberty was. She was wearing a long swimming costume that reached from neck to knees, but she still kept her hat on.

The Alderman had stripped off his long robe and chain, and was sitting on the canal bank in his shirtsleeves and some braces that could have moored a ship. Johnny wondered how the dead changed clothes, or felt the heat, but he supposed it was all habit. If you thought your shirt was off there it was . . . off.

As for swimming . . . there was no splash when they dived, just the faintest of shimmers, that spread out like ripples and vanished very quickly. And when they surfaced they didn't look wet. It dawned on Johnny that when a ghost (he had to use that word in his head) jumped into the water, the ghost didn't get wet, the water got ghostly.

Not all of them were having fun, though. At least, not the usual sort. Mr Fletcher and Solomon Einstein and a few others were clustered around one of the dumped televisions.

'What are they doing?' said Johnny.

'Trying to make it work,' said Mr Vicenti.

Johnny laughed. The screen had been smashed.

Rain had dripped into the case for years. There was even grass growing out of it.

'That'll never—' he began.

There was a crackle. A picture formed in the air, on a *screen that wasn't there any more*.

Mr Fletcher stood up and solemnly shook Solomon Einstein's hand.

'Another successful marriage of advanced theoretics and practical know-how, Mr Einstein.'

'A shtep in the right direction, Mr Fletcher.'

Johnny stared at the flickering images. The picture was in beautiful colour.

Enlightenment dawned.

'It's the *ghost* of the television?' he said.

'Vot a clever boy!' said Solomon Einstein.

'But with *improvements*,' said Mr Fletcher.

Johnny peered inside the case. It was full of old leaves and stained, twisted metal. But over the top of it, shimmering gently, was the pearly outline of the ghost of the machine, purring away without electricity. At least, apparently without electricity. Who knew where the electricity went when the light was switched off?

'Oh, wow.'

He stood up and pointed to the scummy green surface of the canal.

'Somewhere down there there's an old Ford Capri,' he said. 'Wobbler said he saw some men dump it in there once.'

'I shall see to it directly,' said Mr Fletcher. 'The internal combustion engine certainly could do with some improvements.'

'But . . . look . . . machines aren't alive, so how can they have ghosts?'

'But zey have *existence*,' said Einstein. 'From moment to moment. Zo, we find the right moment, yes?'

'Sounds a bit occult,' said Johnny.

'No! It is *physics*! It is *beyond* physics. It is—' he waved both hands excitedly, '*meta*physics. From the Greek *meta*, meaning "beyond", and *physika*, meaning . . . er . . .'

'Physics,' said Mr Vicenti.

'Exactly!'

'Nothing ever finishes. Nothing's ever really over.'

It was Johnny who said that. He was surprised at himself.

'Correct! Are you a physicist?'

'Me?' said Johnny. 'I don't know anything about science!'

'Marvellous! Ideal qualification!' said Einstein.

'What?'

'Ignorance is very important! It is an absolutely *essential* step in the learning process!'

Mr Fletcher twiddled the ghost of a tuning knob.

'Well, we're all right now,' he said, watching a programme in what sounded like Spanish. 'Over here, everyone!'

'How very interesting,' said Mrs Liberty, dressing herself in the blink of an eye. 'Miniature cine-matography?'

When Johnny left they were all in front of the busted television, arguing over what to watch . . .

Except for Mr Grimm. He stood a little apart, hands folded obediently, watching them.

'There will be trouble because of this,' he said. 'This is disobedience. Meddling with the physical.'

He had a small moustache as well as glasses and, in daylight, Johnny saw that the lenses were those thick ones that seem to hide the person's eyes.

'There'll be trouble,' he said again. 'And it will be *your* fault, John Maxwell. You're getting them excited. Is this any way for the dead to behave?'

Two invisible eyes followed him.

'Mr Grimm?' said Johnny.

'Yes?'

'Who are you?'

'That's none of your business.'

'No, but it's just that everyone else always talks about—'

'*I* happen to believe in decency. I believe life should be taken seriously. There is a proper way to conduct oneself. *I* certainly don't intend to indulge in this foolish behaviour.'

'I didn't mean to—'

Mr Grimm turned around and walked stiffly to his little stone under the trees. He sat down with his arms folded, and glared at Johnny.

'No good will come of it,' he said.

He said he'd been to see a specialist. That was always a good one. Teachers generally didn't ask any more questions.

At break, Wobbler had News.

'My mum said there's going to be a big meeting about it in the Civic Centre tonight, with television there and everything.'

'It won't do any good,' said Yo-less. 'It's been going on for ages. It's too late. There's been all kinds of inquiries and stuff.'

133

'I asked my mum about building things on old graveyards and she says they have to get a vicar in to desecrate the site first,' said Wobbler. 'That should be worth seeing.'

'It's *de-consecrate*,' said Yo-less. 'Desecrate is all to do with sacrificing goats and things.'

Wobbler looked wistful.

'I suppose there's no chance—'

'None!'

'I'm going to go along tonight,' said Johnny. 'And you lot ought to come.'

'It won't do any good,' said Yo-less.

'Yes it will,' said Johnny.

'Look, the place has still been sold,' said Yo-less. 'I know you're sort of wound up about it, but it's all over.'

'Going along will still do some good.' He knew it, in the same way he'd known the Pals were important. Not for *reasons*. Just because it was.

'Will there be any . . . freak winds?' said Bigmac.

'How do I know? Shouldn't think so. They're all watching television.'

The other three exchanged glances.

'The *dead* are watching television?' said Wobbler.

'That's right. And I know you're all trying to think of funny things to say. Just don't say them.

They're watching television. They've made an old TV set work.'

'Well, I suppose it passes the time,' said Wobbler.

'I don't think they experience time like we do,' said Johnny.

Yo-less slid down off the wall.

'Talking of time,' he said, 'I'm not sure tomorrow would be a good time to go hanging around cemeteries.'

'Why not?' said Bigmac.

'You know what day it is?'

'Tuesday,' said Johnny.

'Halloween,' said Wobbler. 'You're all coming to my party, remember?'

'Whoops,' said Bigmac.

'The principle is astonishingly simple,' said Mr Fletcher. 'A tiny point of light! That's all it is! Whizzing backwards and forwards inside a glass bottle. Basically it's a thermionic valve. *Much* easier to control than sound waves—'

'Excuse me,' said Mrs Liberty. 'When you stand in front of the screen you make the picture go blurred.'

'Sorry.' Mr Fletcher went back and sat down. 'What's happening now?'

The dead were ranged in rows, fascinated.

'Mr McKenzie has told Dawn that Janine can't go to Doraleen's party,' said William Stickers, without taking his eyes off the screen.

'I must say,' said the Alderman, 'I thought Australia was a bit different. More kangaroos and fewer young women in unsuitable clothing.'

'I'm quite happy with the young women,' said William Stickers.

'Mr Stickers! For shame! You're *dead*!'

'But I have a very good memory, Mrs Liberty.'

'Oh. Is it over?' said Solomon Einstein, as the credits rolled up the screen and the *Cobbers* theme tune rolled over the canal. 'But there iss the mystery of who took the money from Mick's coat!'

'The man in the television just said there will be another performance tomorrow,' said Mrs Liberty. 'We must be sure not to miss it.'

'It is getting dark,' said Mr Vicenti, from the back of the group. 'Time we were getting back.'

The dead looked across at the cemetery.

'If we want to go, that is,' he added. He was smiling faintly.

The dead were silent. Then the Alderman said, 'Well, I'm blowed if I'm going back in there.'

'Thomas Bowler!' snapped Mrs Liberty.

'Well, if a man can't swear when he's dead, it's a poor lookout. Blowed, blowed, blowed. And damn,' said the Alderman. 'I mean, look, will you? There's radio and television and all sorts. There's things going on! I don't see why we should go back in there. It's dull. No way.'

'No way?'

William Stickers nudged Mrs Liberty. 'That's Australian for "certainly not",' he whispered.

'But staying where we're put is *proper*,' said Mrs Liberty. 'We have to stay where we've been *put*—'

'Ahem.'

It was Mr Grimm. The dead looked at their feet.

'I entirely agree,' he said.

'Oh. Hello, Eric,' said the Alderman coldly.

Eric Grimm folded his hands on his chest and beamed at them. This worried even the dead. The thickness of his glasses somehow made his eyes get lost, so that all that was on the other side of them was pinkness.

'Will you listen to what you are saying?' he said. 'You're *dead*. Act your age. It's *over*.' He waved a finger. 'You know what will happen if you leave. You know what will happen if you're too long away. It's dreadful to think about, isn't it? You're letting this idiot child get you all upset.'

The dead tried not to meet his gaze. When you were dead, there were some things that you knew, in the same way that when you were alive you knew about breathing. It was that *a day would come*. And you had to be prepared. There'd be a final sunrise, and you had to face it, and be ready.

A final sunrise. The day of judgement. It could be any day. You had to be ready.

'Not gallivanting off apeing your juniors,' said Mr Grimm, who seemed to read their thoughts. 'We're dead. So we wait here, like decent people. Not go dabbling in the Ordinary.'

The dead shuffled their feet.

'Well, I've waited eighty years,' said the Alderman, at last. 'If it happens tonight, it happens. I'm going to go and have a look around. Anyone else coming?'

'Yes. Me,' said William Stickers, standing up.

'Anyone else?'

About half the dead stood up. A few more looked around and decided to join them. There was something about Mr Grimm that made you want to be on the other side.

'You will get lost!' warned Mr Grimm. 'Something will go wrong, you know! And then you'll be wandering around forever, and you'll . . . forget.'

'I've got descendants out there,' said the Alderman.

'We've all got descendants,' said Mrs Liberty.

'And we know what the rules are. And so do you.' She looked embarrassed.

There *were* rules. You were never told them, any more than you were told that things dropped when you let go of them. They were just *there*.

But the Alderman was unbudgeable in a sullen kind of way.

'At least I'm going to have a look around. Check out my old haunts,' he muttered.

'Haunts?' said William Stickers.

'Check out?' said Mrs Liberty.

'That's modern talk for—' William Stickers began.

'I'm *sure* I *don't* want to know!' Mrs Liberty stood up. 'The very idea!'

'There's a world out there, and we helped to make it, and now I want to find out what it's like,' said the Alderman sulkily.

'Besides,' said Mr Vicenti, 'if we stick together no one will forget who they are, and we'll all go further.'

Mrs Liberty shook her head.

'Well, if you *insist* on going, then I suppose someone with some Sense should accompany you,' she said.

The dead marched off in, as it were, a body, down the canal path and towards the town centre. That left only Mr Einstein and Mr Fletcher, still sitting happily beside their television.

'What's got into them?' said Mr Fletcher. 'They're acting almost *alive*.'

'It is disgusting,' said Mr Grimm, but somehow in a triumphant tone of voice, as if seeing people acting badly was very satisfying.

'Solomon here says that space is a delusion,' said Mr Fletcher. 'Therefore, it is *impossible* to go anywhere. Or to be anywhere, either.'

Einstein spat on his hands and tried to smooth down his hair.

'On ze other hand—' he said, 'there *was* a nice little pub in Cable Street.'

'You wouldn't get a drink, Solly,' said Mr Fletcher. 'They don't serve spirits.'

'I used to like it in there,' said Einstein, wistfully. 'After a hard day stuffing foxes, it wass nice to relax of an evenink.'

'You *did* say space was a delusion,' said Mr

Fletcher. 'Anyway, I thought we were going to do some more work on the television. You said there was no theoretical reason why we shouldn't be able to make—'

'I zink,' said Mr Einstein carefully, 'I would like to fool myself a little.'

And then there was only Mr Grimm.

He turned back, still smiling in a glassy kind of way, and settled down and waited for them to return.

Chapter 7

The Frank W. Arnold Civic Centre meeting room was about half full.

It smelled of chlorine from the swimming baths, and of dust, and floor polish, and wooden chairs. Occasionally people would wander in thinking the meeting was the AGM of the bowls club, and then try to wander out again, pushing on the bar on the door marked 'Pull' and then glaring at it as if only an idiot would put 'Pull' on a door you pulled. The speakers spent a lot of the time asking people at the back if they could hear, and then holding the microphone too close to the loudspeakers, and then someone tried to make the PA system work properly, and blew a fuse, and went to find the caretaker, pushing on the door for a while like a hamster trying to find the way out of its treadmill.

In fact, it was like every other public meeting Johnny had ever attended. Probably on Jupiter seven-legged aliens had meetings in icy halls smelling of chlorine, he thought, with the microphones howling, and creatures frantically ▼Σσaing at doors clearly marked 'βΓπ'.

There were one or two of his teachers in the audience. That was amazing. You never really thought of them doing anything after school. You never knew about people, like you never knew how deep a pond was because all you saw was the top. And he recognized one or two people he'd seen in the cemetery walking their dogs or just sitting on the seats. They looked out of place.

There were a couple of people from United Amalagamated Consolidated Holdings, and a man from the Council planning office, and the chairman of Blackbury Municipal Authority, who looked a lot like Mrs Liberty and turned out to be a Miss Liberty. (Johnny wondered if Mrs Liberty was her great-grandmother or something, but it would be hard to ask; you couldn't very well say, 'Hey, you look like this dead lady, are you related?')

They didn't look out of place. They looked as though they were used to platforms.

Johnny found he couldn't listen to them properly. The pock-pock from the squash court on the
other side of the wall punctuated the sentences
like a rain of full stops, and the rattling of the door
bar was a semi-colon.

'—better. Future. For the young; people of our
city—'

Most of the people in the audience were middle
aged. They listened to all the speakers very
intently.

'—assure the good. People. of Blackbury; that.
We. At United Consolidated; Holdings value.
Public. Opinion most highly; and have no inten-
tion. Of—'

Words poured out. He could feel them filling up
the hall.

And afterwards – he told himself, in the privacy
of his own head – afterwards, the day after tomorrow, the cemetery would be shut, no matter
what anyone said. It'd vanished into the past
just like the old boot factory. And then the past
would be rolled up and tucked away in old newspapers, just like the Pals. Unless someone did
something.

Life was difficult enough already. Let someone
else say something.

'—not even a *particularly* fine example. Of Edwardian funereal sculpture. With—'

The words would fill up the hall until they were higher than people's heads. They were smooth, soothing words. Soon they'd close over the top of all the trilbies and woolly hats, and everyone would be sitting there like sea anemones.

They'd come here with things to say, even if they didn't know how to say them.

The thing was to keep your head down.

But if you *did* keep your head down, you'd drown in other people's words.

'—fully taken into. Account; at every stage of the planning process—'

Johnny stood up, because it was that or drowning. He felt his head break through the tide of words, and he breathed in. And then out.

'Excuse me, please?' he said.

The White Swan in Cable Street, known for years as The Dirty Duck, was a traditional English pub, with a 'Nuke the Gook' video machine that Shakespeare himself might have played. It was crowded, and noisy with electronic explosions and the jukebox.

In one corner, wedged between the video quiz

game and the wall, in a black felt hat, nursing half a pint of Guinness, was mad old Mrs Tachyon.

Mad is a word used about people who've either got no senses or several more than most other people.

Mrs Tachyon was the only one who noticed the drop in temperature. She looked up, and grinned a one-toothed grin.

The patch of chilly air drifted across the crowded room until it came up against the jukebox. Frost steamed off it for a second.

The tune changed.

'"Roses are Blooming in Piccardy",' said Mrs Tachyon happily. 'Yes!'

She watched carefully as people clustered around the machine and started to thump it. Then they pulled the plug, which made no difference.

The barmaid screamed and dropped a tray of drinks when the games machine exploded and caught fire.

Then the lights fused.

A minute or two later, Mrs Tachyon was left in the dark, listening to the barman cursing somewhere in a back room as fuses kept blowing.

It was quite pleasant, sitting in the warm glow of the melted machinery.

From the wreckage on the floor, the ghosts of two pints of beer detached themselves and floated across to the table.

'Cheers!' said Mrs Tachyon.

The chairman of the Council looked over her glasses.

'Questions at the end, please.'

Johnny wavered. But if he sat down, the words would close over his head again.

'When is the end, please?' he said.

Johnny felt everyone looking at him.

The chairman glanced at the other speakers. She had a habit, Johnny noticed, of closing her eyes when she started a sentence and opening them suddenly at the end, so that they'd leap out and surprise you.

'When [close] we've fully. Discussed. The situation. And then I will call for [open!] questions.'

Johnny decided to swim for the shore.

'But I'll have to leave before the end,' he said. 'I have to be in bed by ten.'

There was a general murmur of approval from the audience. It was clear that most of them approved of the idea of anyone under thirty being in bed by ten. It was almost true, anyway. He was generally in his room around ten, although there was no telling when the lights actually went off.

'Let the lad ask his question,' said a voice from near the front.

'He's doing a project,' said another voice. Johnny recognized Mr Atterbury, sitting bolt upright.

'Oh . . . very well. What was it, young man?'

'Um.' Johnny felt them all looking at him. 'Well, the thing is . . . the thing I want to know *is* . . . is there anything that anyone can say here, tonight, that's going to make any difference?'

'That *[close]* hardly seems an appropriate sort of *[open!]* question,' said the chairman severely.

'Seems damned good to me,' said Mr Atterbury. 'Why doesn't the man from United Amalagamated Consolidated Holdings answer the boy? Just a simple answer would do.'

The United man gave Johnny a frank, open smile.

'We shall, of course, take all views very *deeply* into consideration,' he said. 'And—'

'But there's a sign up saying that you're going to build anyway,' said Johnny 'Only I don't think many people want the old cemetery built on. So you'll take the sign down, will you?'

'We have in fact bought the—'

'You paid fivepence,' said Johnny. 'I'll give you a pound.'

People started to laugh.

'I've got a question too,' said Yo-less, standing up.

The chairman, who had her mouth open, hesitated. Yo-less was beaming at her, defying her to tell *him* to sit down.

'We'll take the question from the other young man, the one in the shirt – no, not you, the—' she began.

'The black one,' said Yo-less, helpfully. 'Why did the Council sell the cemetery in the first place?'

The chairman brightened up at this one.

'I *[close]* think we have covered that very fully *[open!]*,' she said. 'The cost of upkeep—'

Bigmac nudged Johnny, pointed at a sheet of figures everyone had been given, and whispered in his ear.

'But I don't see how there's much upkeep in a cemetery,' said Yo-less. 'Sending someone in once or twice a year to cut the brambles down doesn't sound like much of a cost to me.'

'We'd do it for nothing,' said Johnny.

'Would we?' whispered Wobbler, who liked fresh air to be something that happened to other people, preferably a long way off.

People were turning round in their seats.

The chairman gave a loud sigh, to make it clear that Johnny was being just too stupid but that she was putting up with him nevertheless.

'The *fact*, young man, as I have explained time and again, is that it is simply too expensive to maintain a cemetery that is—'

As he listened, red with embarrassment, Johnny remembered about the chance to have another go. He could just put up with it and shut up, and for ever after he'd wonder what would have happened, and then when he died that angel – although, as things were going at the moment, angels were in short supply even after you were dead – would say, hey, would you have liked to have found out what happened? And he'd say yes, really, and the angel would send him back and maybe this *was*—

He pulled himself together.

'No,' he said, 'it isn't simply too expensive.'

The woman stopped in mid-sentence.

'How dare you interrupt me!' she snapped.

Johnny ploughed on. 'It says in your papers here

that the cemetery makes a loss. But a cemetery can't make a loss. It's not like a business or something. It just *is*. My friend Bigmac here says what you're calling a loss is just the value of the land for building offices. It's the rates and taxes you'd get from United Amalagamated Consolidated Holdings. But the dead can't pay taxes so they're not worth anything.'

The man from United Amalagamated Consolidated Holdings opened his mouth to say something, but the chairman stopped him.

'A democratically elected Council—' she began.

'I'd like to raise a few points concerning that,' said Mr Atterbury. 'There are certain things about this sale which I should like to see more clearly explained in a democratic way.'

'I've had a good look round the cemetery, ' said Johnny, plunging on. 'I've been . . . doing a project. I've walked round it a lot. It's full of stuff. It doesn't matter that no one in there is really famous. They were famous *here*. They lived and got on with things and died. They were *people*. It's wrong to think that the past is something that's just gone. It's still there. It's just that *you've* gone past. If you drive through a town, it's still there in the rear-view mirror. Time is a road, but it doesn't roll up behind you. Things aren't over just because they're *past*. Do you see that?'

People told one another that it was getting chilly for the time of year. Little points of coldness drifted around the town.

Screen K at the Blackbury Odeon was showing a 24-hour, non-stop Halloween Special, but people kept coming out. It was too cold in there, they said. And it was creepy. Armpit, the manager, who was one of Wobbler's mortal enemies, and who looked like two men in one dinner jacket, said it was *supposed* to be creepy. They said not *that* creepy. There were voices that you didn't exactly hear, and they – well, you kept getting the impression that people were sitting right beh— Well, let's go and get a burger. Somewhere brightly-lit.

Pretty soon there was hardly anyone in there at all except Mrs Tachyon, who'd bought a ticket because it was somewhere in the warm, and spent most of the time asleep.

'*Elm Street? Elm Street? Wasn't there an Elm Street down by Beech Lane?*'

'*I don't think it was this one. I don't remember this sort of thing going on.*'

She didn't mind the voices at all.

JOHNNY AND THE DEAD

'Freddie. Now that's a NICE name.'

They were company, in a way.

'And that's a nice jumper.'

And a lot of people had left popcorn and things behind in their hurry to get out.

'But I don't think THAT'S very nice.'

The next film was *Ghostbusters*, followed by *Wednesday of the Living Dead*.

It seemed to Mrs Tachyon that the voices, which didn't exist anyway, had gone very quiet.

Everyone was staring at Johnny now.

'And . . . and,' said Johnny, '. . . if we forget about them, we're just a lot of people living in . . . in buildings. We need them to tell us who we are. They built this city. They did all the daft human things that turn a lot of buildings into a place for people. It's wrong to throw all that away.'

The chairman shuffled the papers in front of her.

'Nevertheless *[close]*, we have to deal with the *[open!]* present day,' she said brusquely. 'The dead are no longer here and I am afraid they do not vote.'

'You're wrong. They are here and they have got a vote,' said Johnny. 'I've been working it out. In my head. It's called tradition. And they outvote us twenty to one.'

Everyone went quiet. Nearly as quiet as the unseen audience in Screen K.

Then Mr Atterbury started to clap. Someone else joined in – Johnny saw it was the nurse from Sunshine Acres. Pretty soon everyone was clapping, in a polite yet firm way.

Mr Atterbury stood up again.

'Mr Atterbury, sit down,' said the chairman. 'I am running this meeting, you know.'

'I am afraid this does not appear to be the case,' said Mr Atterbury. 'I'm standing up and I'm going to speak. The boy is right. Too much has been taken away, I do know that. You dug up the High Street. It had a lot of small shops. People lived there. Now it's all walkways and plastic signs and people are afraid of it at night. Afraid of the town where they live! I'd be ashamed of that, if I was you. And we had a coat of arms for the town, up on the Town Hall. Now we've got some kind of plastic logo thing. And you took the old allotments and built the Neil Armstrong Shopping Mall and all the little shops went out of business. And they were beautiful, those allotments.'

'They were a mess!'

'Oh, yes. A beautiful mess. Home-made green-houses made of old window frames nailed together. Old men sitting out in front of their sheds in old chairs. Vegetables and dogs and children all over the place. I don't know where all those people went, do you? And then you knocked down a lot of houses and built the big tower block where no one wants to live and named it after a crook.'

'I didn't even live here in those days,' said the chairman. 'Besides, it's generally agreed that the Joshua N'Clement block was a . . . *misplaced* idea.'

'A bad idea, you mean.'

'Yes, if you must put it like that.'

'So mistakes can be made, can they?'

'Nevertheless, the plain fact is that we have to build for the future—'

'I'm very glad to hear you say that, madam chairman, because I'm sure you'll agree that the most successful buildings have got very deep foundations.'

There was another round of applause. The people on the platform looked at one another.

'I feel I have no alternative but to close the meeting,' said the chairman stiffly. 'This was supposed to be an informative occasion.'

'I think it has been,' said Mr Atterbury.

'But you can't close the meeting,' said Johnny.

'Indeed, I can!'

'You can't,' said Johnny, 'because this is a public hall, and we're all public, and no one's done anything wrong.'

'Then we shall leave, and there will really be no point in the meeting!' said the chairman. She swept up her papers and stalked across the platform, down the steps and across the hall. The rest of the platform party, with one or two helpless glances at the audience, followed her.

She led the way to the door.

Johnny offered up a silent prayer.

Someone, somewhere, heard it.

She pushed when she should have pulled. The rattling was the only noise, and it grew frantic as she began to lose her temper. Finally, one of the men from United Amalagamated Consolidated Holdings yanked the bar and the door jolted open.

Johnny risked looking behind him. He couldn't see anyone who looked dead.

A week ago that would have sounded really *odd*.

It didn't sound much better now.

'I thought I felt a draught,' he said. 'Just now?'

'They've left the windows open at the back,' said Yo-less.

They're not here, Johnny thought. I'm going to have to do this by myself. Oh, well . . .

'Are we going to get into trouble?' said Wobbler. 'This *was* supposed to be a public meeting.'

'Well, we're public, aren't we?' said Johnny.

'Are we?'

'Why not?'

Everyone sat for a while looking at the empty platform. Then Mr Atterbury got up and limped up the steps.

'Shall we have a meeting?' he said.

Cold air swirled out of the cinema.

'Well, THAT was an education.'

'Some of those tricks must have been done with mirrors, if you want MY opinion.'

'What shall we do now?'

'We should be getting back.'

'Back where?'

'Back to the cemetery, of course.'

'Madam, the night is young!'

'That's right! We've only just started enjoying ourselves.'

'Yes! Anyway, you're a long time dead, that's what I always say.'

'I want to get out there and enjoy life. I never enjoyed it much when I WAS alive.'

'*Thomas Bowler! That's no way for a respectable man to behave!*'

The crowd queuing outside the burger bar drew closer together as the chilly wind drove past.

'*Thomas Bowler? Do you know . . . I never really enjoyed being Thomas Bowler.*'

The audience in the Frank W. Arnold Civic Centre looked a bit sheepish, like a class after the teacher has stormed out. Democracy only works very well if people are told how to do it.

Someone raised a hand.

'*Can* we actually stop it happening?' she said. 'It all sounded very . . . official.'

'Officially, I don't think we can,' said Mr Atterbury. 'There was a proper sale. United Amalagamated Consolidated Holdings could get unpleasant.'

'There's plenty of other sites,' said someone else. 'There's the old jam works in Slate Road, and all that area where the old goods yard used to be.'

'And we could give them their money back.'

'We could give them *double* their money back,' said Johnny.

There was more laughter at this.

'It seems to me,' said Mr Atterbury, 'that a

company like United Amalagamated Consolidated
Holdings has to take notice of people. The boot factory never took any notice of people, I do know
that. It didn't have to. It made boots. That was all
there was to it. But no one's quite certain about
what UACH does, so they have to be nice about it.'
He rubbed his chin. 'Big companies like that don't
like *fuss*. And they don't like being laughed at. If
there was another site . . . and if they thought we
were serious . . . and if we threaten to offer them,
yes, double their money back . . .

'And then we ought to do something about the
High Street,' said someone.

'And get some decent playgrounds and things
again, instead of all these Amenities all over the
place.'

'And blow up Joshua N'Clement and get some
proper houses built—'

'Yo!' said Bigmac.

'Here here,' said Yo-less.

Mr Atterbury waved his hands calmly.

'One thing at a time,' he said. 'Let's rebuild
Blackbury first. We can see about Jerusalem
tomorrow.'

'And we ought to find a name for ourselves!'

'The Blackbury Preservation Society?'

'Sounds like something you put in a jar.'

'All right, the Blackbury *Conservation* Society.'

'Still sounds like jam to me.'

'The Blackbury Pals,' said Johnny.

Mr Atterbury hesitated.

'It's a good name,' he said eventually, while lots of people in the hall started asking one another who the Blackbury Pals were. 'But . . . no. Not now. But they were officially the Blackbury Volunteers. That's a good name.'

'But that doesn't say what we're going to do, does it?'

'If we start off not knowing what we're going to do, we could do anything,' said Johnny. 'Einstein said that,' he added, proudly.

'What, Albert Einstein?' said Yo-less.

'No, Solomon Einstein,' said Mr Atterbury. 'Hah! Know about him too, do you?'

'Er . . . yes.'

'I remember him. He used to keep a taxidermist and fishing tackle shop in Cable Street when I was a lad. He was always saying that sort of thing. A bit of a philosopher, was Solomon Einstein.'

'And all he did was stuff things?' said Yo-less.

'*And* think,' said Johnny.

'Well, that kind of cogitation runs in the family,

you might say,' said Mr Atterbury. 'Besides, you've got a lot of time for abstract thought when you've got your hand stuck up a dead badger.'

'Yes, you certainly wouldn't want to think about what you were doing,' said Wobbler.

'Blackbury Volunteers it is, then,' said Mr Atterbury.

Frost formed on the receiver of the public phone in The White Swan.

'*Ready, Mr Einstein?*'

'*Let's go, Mr Fletcher!*'

The telephone clicked, and was silent. The air warmed up again.

Thirty seconds later, the air grew cold in the little wooden hut twenty miles away that housed the controls of Blackbury University's radio telescope.

'*It works!*'

'*Off course. Off all the forces in the universe, the hardest to overcome is the force of habit. Gravity is easy-peasy by comparison.*'

'*When did you think of that?*'

'*It came to me ven I was working on a particularly large trout.*'

'*Really? Well . . . let's see what we can do . . .*'

Mr Fletcher looked around the little room. It was

currently occupied only by Adrian 'Nozzer' Miller, who'd wanted to be an astronomer because he thought it was all to do with staying up late looking through telescopes, and hadn't bargained on it being basically about adding columns of figures in a little shed in the middle of a windy field.

The figures the telescope was producing were all that was left of an exploding star twenty million years ago. A billion small rubbery things on two planets who had been getting on with life in a quiet sort of way had been totally destroyed, but they were certainly helping Adrian get his Ph.D. and, who knows, they might have thought it all worthwhile if anyone had asked them.

He looked up as the telescope motors ground into action. Lights flickered on the control panel.

He stared at the main switches, and then reached out for them. They were so cold they hurt.

'Ow!'

The big dish turned towards the moon, which was just over Blackbury.

There was a clattering from the printer beside him, and the endless stream of paper it was producing now read:

OIOIOIOOIOIOIOIOIOOOIOOOOIOOOOIIOOIIOOOIOIO
HEREGOESNOTHINGGGGooooooooooIIIoIIII
WELLIM*BACK*OOOOIOOOI . . .

Mr Fletcher had just bounced off the moon.

'Vot was it like?'

'I didn't have time to see much, but I don't think I'd like to live there. It worked, though. The sky's the limit, Mr Einstein!'

'Exactly, Mr Fletcher! By the vay, where did that young man go?'

'I think he had to rush off somewhere.'

'Oh. Well . . . we should go and tell the others, don't you think?'

It was a quiet night in Blackbury Central police station. Sergeant Comely had time to sit back and watch the little lights on the radio.

He'd never really been happy about the radio, even when he was younger. It was the bane of his life. He suffered from education, and he'd never been able to remember all that 'Foxtrot Tango Piper' business – at least when he was, e.g., pelting down the street at 2 a.m. in pursuit of miscreants. He'd end up sending messages about 'Photograph

Teapot Psychological'. It had definitely blighted his promotion chances.

He especially hated radio on nights like this, when he was in charge. He hadn't joined the police to be good at technology.

Then the phones started to ring. There was the manager of the Odeon. Sergeant Comely couldn't quite make out what he was saying.

'Yes, yes, all right, Halloween Spectacular,' he said. 'What do you mean, it's all gone cold? What do you want me to do? Arrest a cinema for being cold? I'm a police officer, not a central heating specialist! I don't repair video machines, either!'

The phone rang again as soon as he put it down, but this time one of the young constables answered it.

'It's someone from the university,' he said, putting his hand over the mouthpiece. 'He says a strange alien force has invaded the radio telescope. You know, that big satellite dish thing over towards Slate?'

Sergeant Comely sighed. 'Can you get a description?' he said.

'I saw a film about this, Sarge,' said another policeman. 'These aliens landed and replaced everyone in the town with giant vegetables.'

'Really? Round here it'd be days before anyone noticed,' said the sergeant.

The constable put the phone down.

'He just said it was like a strange alien force,' he said. 'Very cold, too.'

'Oh, a *cold* strange alien force,' said Sergeant Comely.

'And it was invisible, too.'

'Right. Would he recognize it if he didn't see it again?'

The young policemen looked puzzled. I'm too good for this, the sergeant thought.

'All right,' he said. 'So we know the following. Strange invisible aliens have invaded Blackbury. They dropped in at The Dirty Duck, where they blew up the Space Invaders machine, which makes sense. And then they went to the pictures. Well, that makes sense too. It's probably *years* before new films get as far as Alfred Centuri . . .'

The phone rang again. The constable answered it.

'And what, we ask ourselves, is their next course of action?'

'It's the manager of Pizza Surprise, Sarge,' said the constable. 'He says—'

'Right!' said the sergeant. 'That's right! They drop

in for a Number Three with Extra Pepperoni! It probably looks like a friend of theirs.'

'Wouldn't do any harm to go and chat to him,' said the constable. It had been a long time since dinner. 'You know, just to show a bit of—'

'*I'll* go,' said Sergeant Comely, picking up his hat. 'But if I come back as a giant cucumber, there's going to be *trouble*.'

'No anchovies on mine, Sarge,' said the constable, as Sergeant Comely stepped out into the night.

There was something strange in the air. Sergeant Comely had lived in Blackbury all his life, and it had never felt like this. There was an electrical tingle to things, and the air tasted of tin.

It suddenly struck him.

What if it were real? Just because they made silly films about aliens and things didn't actually mean, did it, that it couldn't ever happen? He watched them on late-night television. They always picked small towns to land near.

He shook his head. Nah . . .

William Stickers walked through him.

'You know, you really shouldn't have done that, William,' said the Alderman, as Sergeant Comely hurried away.

'He's nothing but a symbol of the oppression of the proletariat,' said William Stickers.

'You've got to have policemen,' said Mrs Liberty. 'Otherwise people would simply do as they liked.'

'Well, we can't have that, can we?' said Mr Vicenti.

The Alderman looked around at the brightly lit street as they strolled along it. There weren't many living people around, but there were quite a lot of dead ones, looking in shop windows or, in the case of some of the older ones, looking *at* shop windows and wondering what they were.

'I certainly don't remember all these shopkeepers from *my* time,' he said. 'They must have moved in recently. Mr Boots and Mr Mothercare and Mr Spudjulicay.'

'Whom?' said Mrs Liberty.

The Alderman pointed to the sign on the other side of the street.

'Spud-u-like,' said Mr Vicenti. 'Hmm.'

'Is that how you pronounce it?' said the Alderman. 'I thought perhaps he was French. My word. And electric light all over the place. And no horse . . . manure in the streets at *all*.'

'Really!' snapped Mrs Liberty. 'Please remember you are in company with a Lady.'

'That's why he said manure,' said William Stickers, happily.

'And the food!' said the Alderman. 'Hindoo and Chinese! Chicken from Kentucky! And what did you say the stuff was that the clothes are made of?'

'Plastic, I think,' said Mr Vicenti.

'Very colourful and long-lasting,' said Mrs Liberty. 'And many of the girls wear bloomers, too. Extremely practical and emancipated.'

'And many of them are extremely handsome,' said William Stickers.

'And everyone's taller and I haven't seen anyone on crutches,' said the Alderman.

'It wasn't always like this,' said Mr Vicenti. 'The nineteen thirties were rather gloomy.'

'Yes, but now . . .' The Alderman spread his arms and turned around. 'Shops full of cinematography televisions! Bright colours everywhere! Tall people with their own teeth! An age of miracles and wonders!'

'The people don't look very happy,' said Mr Vicenti.

'That's just a trick of the light,' said the Alderman.

It was almost midnight. The dead met in the abandoned arcades of the shopping mall. The grilles were up and locked, but that doesn't matter when you're dead.

'Well, that was fun,' said the Alderman.

'I have to agree,' said Mrs Sylvia Liberty. 'I haven't enjoyed myself so much since I was alive. It's a shame we have to go back.'

The Alderman crossed his arms.

'Go back?' he said.

'Now, then, Thomas,' said Mrs Liberty, but in a rather softer voice than she'd used earlier that evening, 'I don't want to sound like Eric Grimm, but you know the rules. We have to return. *A day will come.*'

'I'm not going back. I've really enjoyed *myself*. I'm *not* going back!'

'Me neither,' said William Stickers. 'Down with tyranny!'

'We must be ready for Judgement Day,' said Mrs Liberty. 'You never can tell. It could be tomorrow. Supposing it happened, and we missed it?'

'Hah!' said William Stickers.

'More than eighty years I've been sitting there,' said Alderman Bowler. 'You know, I wasn't expecting that. I thought things went dark for a moment and then there was a man handing out harps.'

'For shame!'

'Well, isn't that what *you* expected?' he demanded.

'Not me,' said William Stickers. 'Belief in the survival of what is laughably called the soul after death is a primitive superstition which has no place in a dynamic socialist society!'

They looked at him.

'You don't think,' said Solomon Einstein, carefully, 'that it is worth reconsidering your opinions in the light of experiental evidence?'

'Don't think you can get round me just because you're accidentally right! Just because I happen to find myself still . . . basically here,' said William Stickers, 'does *not* invalidate the general theory!'

Mrs Liberty banged her phantom umbrella on the floor.

'I won't say it hasn't been enjoyable,' she said, 'but the rules are that we must be back in our places at dawn. Supposing we stayed away too long and forgot who we were? Supposing tomorrow was Judgement Day?'

Thomas Bowler sighed.

'Well, supposing it is?' he said. 'You know what I'd say? I'd say: I did the best I could for eighty-four years. And no one ever told me that afterwards I'd still be this fat old man who gets out of breath. Why do I get out of breath? I don't *breathe*. I passed away, and next thing I knew I was sitting in a marble hut like a man waiting an *extremely long time* for an appointment with the doctor. For nearly ninety years! I'd say: you call this justice? Why are we waiting? *A day will come*. We all . . . arrive knowing it, but no one says when! Just when I was beginning to enjoy life,' he said. 'I wish this night would never end.'

Mr Fletcher nudged Solomon Einstein.

'Shall we tell them?' he said.

'Tell us what?' said William Stickers.

'Vell, you see—' Einstein began.

'Times have changed,' said Mr Fletcher. 'All that stuff about being home at dawn and not hearing the cock crow and stuff like that. That was all very well once upon a time, when people thought the Earth was flat. But no one believes that now—'

'Er—' One of the dead raised a hand.

'Oh, yes,' said Mr Fletcher. 'Thank you, Mr Ronald Newton (1878–1934), former chairman of the Blackbury Flat Earth Society. I know you have Views. But the point I'm trying to make is—'

'—dawn is a place as well as a time,' said Einstein, spreading his hands.

'What on earth do you mean?' said Mrs Liberty.

'On Earth, and around earth,' said Einstein, getting excited. 'One night and one day, forever chasing one another.'

'There is a night that never comes to an end,' said Mr Fletcher. 'All you need is speed . . .'

'Relatively speaking,' said Einstein.

Chapter 8

There is a night that never comes to an end . . .

The clock of the world turns under its own shadow. Midnight is a moving place, hurtling around the planet at a thousand miles an hour like a dark knife, cutting slices of daily bread off the endless loaf of Time.

Time passes everywhere. But days and nights are little local things that happen only to people who stay in one place. If you go fast enough, you can overtake the clock . . .

'How many of us are in this phone box?' said Mr Fletcher.

'Seventy-three,' said the Alderman.

'Very well. Where shall we go? Iceland? It's not even midnight yet in Iceland.'

'Can we have fun in Iceland?' said the Alderman.

173

'How do you feel about fish?'

'Can't abide fish.'

'Not Iceland, then. I believe it's very hard to have fun in Iceland without fish being involved in some way. Well, now . . . it'll be early evening in New York.'

'America?' said Mrs Liberty. 'Won't we get scalped?'

'Good grief; no!' said William Stickers, who was a bit more up to date about the world.

'*Probably* not,' said Mr Fletcher, who had been watching the news lately and was even more up to date than William Stickers.

'Look, we're *dead*,' said the Alderman. 'What else have we got to worry about?'

'Now, this may strike you as an unusual means of travel,' said Mr Fletcher, as something in the telephone began to click, 'but all you have to do, really, is follow me. Incidentally, is Stanley Roundway here?'

The footballer raised his hand.

'We're going *west*, Stanley. For once in your death, try to get the directions right. And now . . .'

One by one, they vanished.

*

Johnny lay in bed, watching the stricken shuttle turning gently in the moonlight.

It had been quite busy after the meeting. Someone from the *Blackbury Guardian* had talked to him, and then Mid-Midlands TV had filmed him, and people had shaken his hand, and he hadn't got home until nearly eleven.

There hadn't been any trouble over that, at least. His mum hadn't come in yet and Grandad was watching a programme about bicycle racing in Germany.

He kept thinking about the Pals. They'd come all the way from France. Yet the dead in the cemetery were so frightened of moving. But they were all the same type of people, really. There had to be a reason for that.

The dead in the cemetery just hung around. Why? The Pals had marched from France, because it was the right thing to do. You didn't have to stay where you were put.

'*New York, New York.*'

  '*Why did they name it twice?*'

  '*Well, they ARE Americans. I suppose they wanted to be sure.*'

  '*The lights are extremely plentiful. What's that?*'

'*The Statue of Liberty.*'

'*Looks a bit like you, Sylvia.*'

'*Sauce!*'

'*Is everyone keeping a look out for those Ghost-breakers?*'

'*I think that was just cinematography, William.*'

'*How long to morning?*'

'*Hours, yet! Follow me, everyone! Let's get a better view!*'

No one ever did work out why all the elevators in the Empire State Building went up and down all by themselves for almost an hour . . .

October the 31st dawned foggy. Johnny wondered about having a one-day illness in preparation for what he suspected was going to be a busy evening, but decided to go to school instead. They always felt happier if you dropped in sometimes.

He went via the cemetery.

There wasn't a living soul. He hated it when it was like this. It was like the bits in the film when you were waiting for the aliens to jump out.

Somehow, they were always more dreadful than the bits with the fangs in.

Then he found Mr Grimm. Anyone else walking along the towpath would have just seen the busted set. But Johnny saw the little man in his neat suit, watching the ghost of the television.

'Ah, boy,' he said. 'You have been causing trouble, have you?' He pointed to the screen.

Johnny gasped. There was Mr Atterbury, very calmly talking to a lady on a sofa. There was also one of the people from United Amalagamated Consolidated Holdings. And he was having some difficulty, was the Consolidated man. He'd come along with some prepared things to say and he was having problems getting his mind round the idea that they weren't working any more.

Mr Grimm turned up the volume control.

'—at every stage, fully sensitive to public opinion in this matter, I can assure you, but there is no doubt that we entered into a proper and legal contract with the relevant Authority.'

'But the Blackbury Volunteers say too much was decided behind closed doors,' said the lady, who looked as though she was enjoying herself. 'They say things were never fully discussed and that no one listened to the local people.'

'Of course, this is not the fault of United Amalagamated Consolidated Holdings,' said Mr Atterbury, smiling benevolently. 'They have an enviable record of civic service and co-operation with the public. I think what we have here is a mistake rather than any *near-criminal activity*, and we in the Volunteers would be more than happy to assist them in any constructive way and, indeed, possibly even compensate them.'

Probably no one else but Johnny and the Consolidated man noticed Mr Atterbury take a ten-pence piece out of his pocket. He turned it over and over in his fingers. The man from the company watched it like a mouse might watch a cat.

He's going to offer him double his money back, Johnny thought. Right there on television.

He didn't. He just kept turning the coin over and over, so that the man could see it.

'That seems a very diplomatic offer,' said the interviewer. 'Tell me, Mr – er—'

'A spokesman,' said the Consolidated man. He looked quite ill. There was a glint as light flashed off the coin.

'Tell me, Mr Spokesman . . . what is it that United Amalagamated Consolidated Holdings actually *does*?'

Mr Atterbury would probably have been a good man in the Spanish Inquisition, Johnny told himself.

Mr Grimm turned the sound down again.

'Where's everyone else?' said Johnny.

'Haven't come back,' said Mr Grimm, with horrible satisfaction. 'Their graves haven't been slept in. *That's* what happens when people don't listen. And do you know what's going to *happen* to them?'

'No.'

'They're going to *fade away*. Oh, yes. You've put ideas in their heads. They think they can go gadding about. But people who go gadding about and not staying where they're put . . . they don't come back. And that's an *end* to it. It could be Judgement Day tomorrow, and they won't be here. Hah! Serves them right.'

There was something about Mr Grimm that made Johnny want to hit him, except that it wouldn't work anyway and, besides, hitting him would be like hitting mud. You'd get dirtier for doing it.

'I don't know where they've gone,' he said, 'but I don't think anything bad's happened to them.'

'Think what you like,' said Mr Grimm, turning back to the television.

'Did you know it's Halloween?' said Johnny.

'Is it?' said Mr Grimm, watching an advert for chocolate. 'I shall have to be careful tonight, then.'

When Johnny reached the bridge he looked back. Mr Grimm was still there, all alone.

*

The dead rode a radio signal over Wyoming . . .

They were already changing. They were still recognizable, but only when they thought about it.

'*You see, I told you it was possible*,' said the person who was occasionally Mr Fletcher. '*We don't need wires!*'

They ran into an electric storm high over the Rocky Mountains. That was fun.

And then they surfed down the radio waves to California.

'*What time is it?*'

'*Midnight!*'

Johnny was a sort of hero in school. The *Blackbury Guardian* had a front page story headed: COUNCIL SLAMMED IN CEMETERY SALE RUMPUS. The *Guardian* often used words like 'slammed' and 'rumpus'; you wondered how the editor talked at home.

Johnny was in the story with his name spelled wrong, and there was a quote which ran: 'War hero Arthur Atterbury, president of the newly formed "Blackbury Volunteers", told the *Guardian*: "There are young people in this town with more sense of history in their little fingers than some adults have in their entire committee-bound bodies". This is thought to be a reference to Cllr Miss Ethel Liberty, who was not available for comment last night.'

Even one or two of the teachers mentioned it; it was unusual for people from the school to appear in the paper; except very close to headlines like TWO FINED AFTER JOYRIDE ESCAPADE.

Even the History master asked him about the Blackbury Pals. And then Johnny found himself telling the class about the Alderman and William Stickers and Mrs Sylvia Liberty, although he said he'd got the information out of the library. One of the girls said she was definitely going to do a project on Mrs Liberty, Champion of Women's Rights, and Wobbler said, yes, champion of women's right to get things wrong, and that started a good argument which lasted until the end of the lesson.

Even the headmaster took an interest – probably out of aforesaid relief that Johnny wasn't involved in one of those YOUTH GANG FINED FOR SHOPLIFTING stories. Johnny had to find his way to his office. The recommended method was to tie one end of a piece of string to somewhere you knew and get your friends to come and look for you if you were away more than two days. He got a short speech about 'social awareness', and was out again a minute later.

He met the other three in the lunch break.

'Come on,' he said.

'Where to?'

'The cemetery. I think something's gone wrong.'

'I haven't had my lunch yet,' said Wobbler. 'It's very important for me to have regular meals. Otherwise my stomach acid plays up.'

'Oh, shut up.'

By the time they raced one another across the heart of Australia, they didn't even need the radio.

The dawn dragged its slow way across the Pacific after them, but they were running free.

'Do we ever need to stop?'

'No!'

'I always wanted to see the world before I died!'

'Well, then, it was just a matter of timing.'

'What time is it?'

'Midnight!'

The cemetery wasn't empty now. There were a couple of photographers there, for one thing, including one from a Sunday newspaper. There was a film crew from Mid-Midlands Television. And the dog-walking people had been joined by others, just walking around and looking.

In a neglected corner, Mrs Tachyon was industri-
ously Vim-ing a gravestone

'Never seen so many people here,' said Johnny.
He added, 'At least, ones who're breathing.'

Yo-less wandered over from where he'd been
talking to a couple of enthusiastic people in
woolly bobble hats, who were peering through the
huge thicket behind Mrs Liberty's grave.

'They say we've not only got environment
and ecology, but some habitat as well,' he said.
'They think they've seen a rare Scandinavian
thrush.'

'Yeah, full of life, this place,' said Bigmac.

A Council lorry had driven a little way up the
towpath. Some men in donkey jackets were har-
vesting the old mattresses. The zombie television
had already gone. Mr Grimm was nowhere to be
seen, even by Johnny.

And a police car was parked just outside the
gates. Sergeant Comely was working on the general assumption that where you got lots of people
gathered together, something illegal was bound to
happen sooner or later.

The cemetery was alive.

'They've gone,' said Johnny. 'I can feel them . . .
not here.'

The other three found that, quite by accident, they'd all moved closer together.

A rare Scandinavian thrush, unless it was a rook, cawed in the elms.

'Gone where?' said Wobbler.

'I don't know!'

'I knew it! I *knew* it!' said Wobbler. 'His eyes'll start to glow any minute, you watch. You've let 'em out! There'll be lurchin' goin' on before this day's over, you wait and see!'

'Mr Grimm said that if they're away too long, they . . . they forget who they were . . .' said Johnny, uncertainly.

'See? See?' said Wobbler. 'You laughed at me! Maybe they're OK when they're remembering who they were, but once they forget . . .'

'*Night of the Killer Zombies*?' said Bigmac.

'We've been through all that,' said Johnny. 'They're *not* zombies!'

'Yeah, but maybe they've been eating voodoo fish and chips,' said Bigmac.

'They're just *not here*.'

'Then where are they?'

'I *don't know*!'

'And it's Halloween, too,' moaned Wobbler.

Johnny walked over to the fence around the old

boot works. There were quite a few cars parked there. He could see the tall thin figure of Mr Atterbury, talking to a group of men in grey suits.

'I wanted to tell them,' he said. 'I mean, we might *win*. Now. People are here. There's TV and everything. Last week it looked hopeless and now there's just a chance and last night I wanted to tell them and now they've gone! And this was their home!'

'Perhaps all these people have frightened them away,' said Yo-less.

'*Day of the Living*,' said Bigmac.

'I should have had my lunch!' said Wobbler. 'My stomach's definitely playing up!'

'They're probably waiting under your bed,' said Bigmac.

'I'm not scared,' said Wobbler. 'I've just got a stomach upset.'

'We ought to be getting back,' said Yo-less. 'I've got to do a project on projects.'

'What?' said Johnny.

'It's for Maths,' said Yo-less. 'How many people in the school are doing projects. That kind of stuff. Statistics.'

'I'm going to look for them,' said Johnny.

'You'll get into trouble when they do the register.'

'I'll say I've been doing something . . . social. That'll probably work. Anyone coming with me?'

Wobbler looked at his feet, or where his feet would be if Wobbler wasn't in the way.

'What about you, Bigmac? You've got your Everlasting Note, haven't you?'

'Yeah, but it's going a bit yellow now . . .'

No one knew when it had been written. Rumour had it that it had been handed down through the generations in Bigmac's family. It was in three pieces. But it generally worked. Although Bigmac kept tropical fish and generally out of trouble, there was something about the way he looked and the way he lived in the Joshua N'Clement block that saw to it no teacher ever questioned the Note, which excused him from doing everything.

'Anyway, they could be anywhere,' he said. 'Anyway, I can't *look* for 'em, can I? Anyway, they're probably just inside your head.'

'You heard them on the radio!'

'I heard *voices*. That's what radio's for, innit?'

It occurred to Johnny, not for the first time, that the human mind, of which each of his friends was in possession of one almost standard sample, was like a compass. No matter how much you shook it up, no matter what happened to it, sooner or later it'd carry on pointing the same way. If three-metre-tall green Martians landed on the shopping mall, bought some greetings cards and a bag of sugar cookies and then took off again, within a day or two people would believe it never happened.

'Not even Mr Grimm's here, and he's *always* here,' said Johnny.

He looked at Mr Vicenti's ornate grave. Some people were taking photographs of it.

'Always here,' he said.

'He's gone weird again,' said Wobbler.

'You all go back,' said Johnny, quietly. 'I just thought of something.'

They all looked round. Their *brains* don't believe in the dead, Johnny thought, but they keep getting outvoted by all the rest of them.

'I'm OK,' said Johnny. 'You go on back. I'll see you at Wobbler's party tonight, all right?'

'Remember not to bring any . . . you know . . . friends,' said Wobbler, as the three of them left.

Johnny wandered down North Drive.

He'd never *tried* to talk to the dead. He'd said things when he knew they were listening, and sometimes they'd been clearly visible, but apart from that first time, when he'd knocked on the door of the Alderman's mausoleum for a joke . . .

'Will you look at this?'

One of the people who'd been examining the grave had picked up the radio, which had been lodged behind a tuft of grass.

'Honestly, people have no respect.'

'Does it work?'

It didn't. A couple of days of damp grass had done for the batteries.

'No.'

'Give it to the men dumping the rubbish on the lorry, then.'

'I'll do it,' said Johnny.

He hurried off with it, keeping a lookout, trying to find one dead person among the living.

'Ah, Johnny.'

It was Mr Atterbury, leaning over the wall of the old boot works. 'Exciting day, isn't it? You started something, eh?'

'Didn't mean to,' said Johnny, automatically. Things were generally his fault.

'It could go either way,' said Mr Atterbury. 'The old railway site isn't so good, but . . . things look promising, I do know that. People have woken up.'

'That's true. A *lot* of people.'

'United Consolidated don't like fuss. The District

Auditor is here, and a man from the Development Commission. It could go very well.'

'Good. Um.'

'Yes?'

'I saw you on television,' said Johnny. 'You called United Consolidated public-spirited and cooperative.'

'Well, they might be. If they've got no choice. They're a bit shifty but we might win through. It's amazing what you can do with a kind word.'

'Oh. Right. Well, then . . . I've got to go and find someone, if you don't mind . . .'

There was no sign of Mr Grimm anywhere. Or any of the others. Johnny hung around for hours, with the birdwatchers and the people from the Blackbury Wildlife Trust, who'd found a fox's den behind William Stickers' memorial, and some Japanese tourists. No one quite knew why the Japanese tourists were there, but Mrs Liberty's grave was getting very well photographed.

Eventually, though, even Japanese tourists run out of film. They took one last shot of themselves in front of William Stickers' monument, and headed back towards their coach.

The cemetery emptied. The sun began to set over the carpet warehouse.

Mrs Tachyon went past with her loaded shopping trolley to wherever it was she spent her nights.

The cars left the old boot works, and only the bulldozers were left, like prehistoric monsters surprised by a sudden cold snap.

Johnny sidled up to the forlorn little stone under the trees.

'I know you're here,' he whispered. 'You can't leave like the others. *You* have to stay. Because *you're* a ghost. A real ghost. You're still here, Mr Grimm. You're not just hanging around like the rest of them. *You're* haunting.'

There was no sound.

'What did you do? Were you a murderer or something?'

There was still no sound. In fact, there was even more silence than before.

'Sorry about the television,' said Johnny nervously.

More silence, so heavy and deep it could have stuffed mattresses.

He walked away, as fast as he dared.

Chapter 9

'This fuss over the cemetery's certainly breathed a bit of life into this town,' said his mother. 'Go and give your grandad his tray, will you? And tell him about it. You know he takes an interest.'

Grandad was watching the News in Hindi. He didn't want to. But the thingy for controlling the set had got lost and everyone had forgotten how to change channels without it.

'Brought you your tray, Grandad.'

'Right.'

'You know the old cemetery? Where you showed me William Stickers' grave?'

'Right.'

'Well, maybe it won't be built on now. There was a meeting last night.'

'Right?'

'I spoke up at the meeting.'

'Right.'

'So it might be all right.'

'Right.'

Johnny sighed. He went back into the kitchen.

'Can I have an old sheet, Mum?'

'What on earth for?'

'Wobbler's Halloween party. I can't think of anything else.'

'There's the one I used as a dust cover, if you're going to cut holes in it.'

'Thanks, Mum.'

'It's pink.'

'Aaaaooow, Mum!'

'It's practically washed out. No one'll notice.' It also, as it turned out, had the remains of some flowers embroidered on one end. Johnny did his best with a pair of scissors.

He'd promised he'd go. But he went the long way round, with the sheet in a bag, just in case the dead had come back and might see him. And there was Mr Grimm to think about now.

After he'd been gone a few minutes, the TV started showing the News in English, which looked less interesting than the Hindi News.

Grandad watched it for a while, and then sat up.
'Hey, girl, it says they're trying to save the old
cemetery.'

'Yes, Dad.'

'It looked like our Johnny on the stage there.'

'Yes, Dad.'

'No one tells me anything around here. What's
this?'

'Chicken, Dad.'

'Right.'

They were somewhere in the high plateaus of
Asia, where once camel trains had traded silk
across five thousand miles and now madmen with
guns shot one another in the various names of
God.

'*How far to morning?*'

'*Nearly there . . .*'

'*What?*'

The dead slowed down in a mountain pass, full
of driving snow.

'*We owe the boy something. He took an interest. He
remembered us.*'

'*Zat's absolutely correct. Conservation of energy. Besides,
he'll be worrying.*'

'*Yes, but . . . if we go back now . . . we'll become like we*' *were, won't we? I can feel the weight of that gravestone now.'*

'Sylvia Liberty! You said we shouldn't leave!'

'I've changed my mind, William.'

'Yes. I spent half my life being frightened of dying, and now I'm dead I'm going to stop being frightened,' said the Alderman. *'Besides . . . I'm remembering things . . .'*

There was a murmur from the rest of the dead.

'I think ve all are,' said Solomon Einstein. *'All the zings we forgot when we were alive . . .'*

'That's the trouble with life,' said the Alderman. *'It takes up your whole time. I mean, I won't say it wasn't fun. Bits of it. Quite a lot of it, really. In its own way. But it wasn't what you'd call living . . .'*

'We don't have to be frightened of the morning,' said Mr Vicenti. *'We don't have to be frightened of anything.'*

A skeleton opened the door.

'It's me, Johnny.'

'It's me, Bigmac. What're you, a gay ghost?'

'It's not that pink.'

'The flowers are good.'

'Come on, let me in, it's freezing out here.'

'Can you float and mince at the same time?'

'Bigmac!'

'Come on, then.'

Somehow, it looked as if Wobbler hadn't really put his heart into the decorations. There were a few streamers and some rubber spiders around the place, and a bowl of the dreadful punch you always get in these circumstances (the one with the brownish bits of orange in it) and bowls full of nibbles with names like Curly-Wigglies. And a vegetable marrow that looked as though it had walked into a combine harvester.

'It was *sposed* to be a Jack-o'-Lantern,' Wobbler kept telling everyone, 'but I couldn't find a pumpkin.'

'Met Hannibal Lecter in a dark alley, did it?' said Yo-less.

'The plastic bats are good, aren't they,' said Wobbler. 'They cost fifty pence each. Have some more punch?'

There were other people there, too, although in the semi-darkness it was hard to make out who they thought they were. There was someone with a lot of stitches and a bolt through his neck, but that was only Nodj, who looked like that anyway. There were a bunch from Wobbler's computer group, who could get drunk on non-alcoholic alcohol and would then stagger around saying things like, 'I'm totally *mad*!' There were a couple of girls

Wobbler vaguely knew. It was that sort of party. You just knew someone would put something daft in the punch, and everyone would talk about school, and one of the girls' dads'd turn up at eleven o'clock and hang around looking determined and put a damper on things, as if they weren't soaking wet already.

'We could play a game,' said Bigmac.

'Not Dead Man's Hand,' said Wobbler. 'Not after last year. You're supposed to pass around grapes and stuff, not just anything you find in the fridge.'

'It wasn't what it *was*,' said one of the girls. 'It was what he *said* it was.'

'All right,' said Johnny to Yo-less, 'I've been trying to work it out. Who are *you*?'

Yo-less had covered half his face with white make-up. He wasn't wearing a shirt, just his ordinary string vest, but he'd found a piece of fake leopard-skin-pattern material which he'd draped over his shoulders. And he had a black hat.

'Baron Samedi, the voodoo god,' said Yo-less. 'I got the idea out of James Bond.'

'That's racial stereotyping,' someone said.

'No, it's not,' said Yo-less. 'Not if *I'm* doing it.'

'I'm pretty sure Baron Samedi didn't wear a

bowler hat,' said Johnny. 'I'm pretty sure it was a top hat. A bowler hat makes you look a bit like you're going to an office somewhere.'

'I can't help it, it was all I could get.'

'Maybe he's Baron Samedi, the voodoo god of chartered accountancy,' said Wobbler.

For a moment Johnny thought of Mr Grimm; his face was all one colour, but he looked like a voodoo god of chartered accountancy if ever there was one.

'In the film he was all mixed up with tarot cards and stuff,' said Bigmac.

'Not really,' said Johnny, waking up. 'Tarot cards are European occult. Voodoo is African occult.'

'Don't be daft, it's American,' said Wobbler.

'No, American occult is Elvis Presley not being dead and that sort of thing,' said Yo-less. 'Voodoo is basically West African with a bit of Christian influence. I looked it up.'

'I've got some *ordinary cards*,' said Wobbler.

'No messing around with cards,' said Baron Yo-less severely. 'My mum'd go spare.'

'What about the thing with the letters and glasses?'

'The postman?'

'You know what I mean.'

'No. That could lead to dark forces taking over,' said Baron Yo-less. 'It's as bad as ouija boards.'

Someone put on a tape and started to dance. Johnny stared into his glass of horrible punch. There was an orange pip floating in it.

Cards and boards, he thought. And the dead. That's not dark forces. Making a fuss about cards and heavy metal and going on about Dungeons and Dragons stuff because it's got demon gods in it is like guarding the door when *it* is really coming up through the floorboards. Real dark forces . . . aren't dark. They're sort of grey, like Mr Grimm. They take all the colour out of life; they take a town like Blackbury and turn it into frightened streets and plastic signs and Bright New Futures and towers where no one wants to live and no one really *does* live. The dead seem more alive than us. And everyone becomes grey and turns into numbers and then, somewhere, someone starts to do arithmetic . . .

The Demon God Yoth-Ziggurat might want to chop your soul up into little pieces, but at least he doesn't tell you that you haven't got one.

And at least you've got half a chance of finding a magic sword.

He kept thinking about Mr Grimm. Even the dead kept away from him.

He woke up to hear Wobbler say, 'We could go Trick or Treating.'

'My mother says that's no better than begging,' said Yo-less.

'Hah, it's worse than that around Joshua N'Clement,' said Bigmac. 'It's called, "Giss five quid or kiss your tyres night-night".'

'We could do it around here,' said Wobbler. 'Or we could go down the mall.'

'That'll just be full of kids in costume running around screaming.'

'A few more won't hurt, then,' said Johnny.

'All right, then, everybody,' Wobbler said. 'Come on . . .'

In fact Neil Armstrong Mall was full of all the other people who'd run out of ideas at Halloween parties. They wandered around in groups looking at one another's clothes and talking, which was pretty much what people did normally in any case, except that tonight the mall looked like Transylvania on late-shopping night.

Zombies lurched under the sodium lights. Witches walked around in groups and giggled at the boys. Grinning pumpkins bobbed on the escalators. Vampires gibbered among the sad indoor trees, and kept fumbling their false fangs back in. Mrs Tachyon rummaged for tins in the litter bins.

Johnny's pink ghost outfit caused a lot of interest.

'Seen any dead around lately?' said Baron Yo-less, when Wobbler and Bigmac had gone off to buy some snacks.

'Hundreds,' said Johnny.

'You know what I mean.'

'No. Not *them*.'

'I'm worried something may have happened to them.'

'They're *dead*. If they exist, that is,' said Yo-less. 'It's not as though they could get run over or something. If you've saved their cemetery for them, they probably just aren't bothering to talk to you any more. That's probably what it is. I think—'

'Anyone want a raspberry snake?' said Wobbler, rustling a large paper bag. 'The skulls are good, too.'

'I'm going home,' said Johnny. 'There's something wrong, and I don't know what it is.'

A ten-year-old Bride of Dracula flapped past.

'I've got to admit, this isn't big fun,' said Wobbler. 'Tell you what . . . there's *Night of the Vampire Nerds* on TV. We could go and watch that.'

'What about everyone else?' said Bigmac. The rest of the party had drifted off.

'Oh, well, they know where I live,' said Wobbler philosophically, as a blood-streaked ghoul went by eating an ice cream.

'I don't believe in vampire nerds,' said Bigmac, as they stepped into the night air. It was a lot colder now, and the mist was coming back.

'Oh, I dunno,' said Wobbler. 'It's the sort we'd have round here.'

'They'd suck fruit juice,' said Yo-less.

'Their mum'd make them go to bed late,' said Bigmac, but they had to think about that.

'Why are we going this way?' said Wobbler. 'This isn't the way back.'

'It's foggy, too,' said Bigmac.

'It's just the mist off the canal,' said Johnny.

Wobbler stopped.

'Oh, no,' he said.

'It's quicker this way,' said Johnny.

'Oh, yes. *Quicker*. Oh, yes. Because I'm gonna *run*!'

'Don't be daft.'

'It's Halloween!'

'So what? You're dressed up as Dracula – what're you worried about!'

'I'm not going past there tonight!'

'It's no different than going past during the day.'

'All right, it's the same, but *I'm* different!'

'Scared?' said Bigmac.

'What? Me? Scared? Huh? Me? I'm not *scared*.'

'Actually, it is a bit risky,' said Baron Yo-less.

'Yes, risky,' said Wobbler hurriedly.

'I mean, you never know,' said Yo-less.

'Never know,' Wobbler echoed.

'Look, it's a street in our town. There's lights and a phone box and everything,' said Johnny. 'I just . . . I won't be happy until I've checked, OK? Anyway, there's four of us, after all.'

'That just means something bad can happen four times,' said Wobbler.

But they'd been walking as they talked; now the little light in the phone box loomed in the fog like a blurred star.

The other three went quiet. The fog hushed all sounds.

Johnny listened. There wasn't even that blotting-paper silence that the dead made.

'See?' he whispered. 'I said—'

Someone coughed, a long way off. All four boys suddenly tried to occupy the same spot.

'Dead people don't cough!' hissed Johnny.

'Then someone's in the cemetery!' said Yo-less.

'Body snatchers!' said Wobbler.

'Burke 'n Head!' said Bigmac.

'I've read about this in the papers!' whispered Wobbler. 'People digging up graves for satanic rites!'

'Shutup!' said Johnny. They sagged. 'Sounded to me like it came from the old boot factory,' he said.

'But it's the middle of the night,' said Yo-less.

They crept forward. There was a dim shape pulled on to the pavement where the streetlights barely shone.

'It's a van,' said Johnny. 'There. Count Dracula never drove a van.'

Bigmac tried to grin. 'Unless he was a Vanpire—'

There was a metallic *clink* somewhere in the fog.

'Wobbler?' said Johnny, in what he hoped was a calm voice.

'Yes?'

'You said you were going to run. Go round to Mr Atterbury's house right now and tell him to come here.'

203

'What? By myself?'

'You'll run faster if you're by yourself.'

'Right!'

Wobbler gave them a frightened look and vanished.

'What, exactly, are we doing?' said Yo-less, as the other three peered into the fog.

There was no mistaking the noise this time. It was wrapped about with fog, but it was definitely the sound of a big diesel engine starting up.

'Someone's nicking a bulldozer!' said Bigmac.

'I wish that's what they were doing,' said Johnny, 'but I don't think they are. Come on, will you?'

'Listen, if someone's driving a bulldozer without lights in the fog, I'm not hanging around!' said Yo-less.

Lights came on, fifty metres away. They didn't show much. They just lit up two cones of fog.

'Is that better?' said Johnny.

'No.'

The lights ground forward. The machine was bumping towards the cemetery railings. Old buddleia bushes and dead stinging nettles smashed under the treads, and there was a clang as the blade hit the low wall.

Johnny ran alongside the machine and shouted, 'Oi!'

The engine stopped.

'Run away!' hissed Johnny to Yo-less. 'Go on! Tell someone what's happening!'

A man unfolded himself from the cab and jumped down. He advanced towards the boys, waving a finger.

'You kids,' he said, 'are in *real* trouble.'

Johnny backed away, and someone grabbed his shoulders.

'You heard the man,' said a voice by his ear. 'It's your fault, this. So you'd better not have seen anything, right? Because we know where you live— Oh, no you don't.' A hand shot out and grabbed Yo-less as he tried to back away.

'Know what I think?' said the man who had been driving the bulldozer. '*I* think it's lucky we happened to be passing and found 'em messing around, eh? Shame they'd driven it right through the place already, eh? Kids today, eh?'

A half-brick sailed past Johnny's face and hit the man beside him on the shoulder.

'What the—'

'*I'll smash your ★★★★ head in! I'll smash your ★★★★ head in!*'

Bigmac emerged from the fog. He looked terrifying. He reached beside him, yanked a railing from the broken wall and started to whirl it round his head as he advanced.

'*You what? You what? You what? I'm MENTAL, me!*'

Then he started to run forward.

'*Aaaaaaarrrrrr—*'

And it dawned on all four people at once that he wasn't going to stop.

Chapter 10

Bigmac bounded over the rubble, an enraged skin-head skeleton.

'Get him!'

'*You* get him!'

The railing smacked into the side of the bull-dozer, and Bigmac leapt.

Even fighting mad, he was still Bigmac, and the driver was a large man. But what Bigmac had going for him was that he was, just for a few seconds, unstoppable. If the man had managed to get one good punch in that would have been it, but there seemed to be too many arms and legs in the way, and also Bigmac was trying to bite his ear.

Even so—

But a pair of headlights appeared near the gate

and started to bounce up and down in a way that suggested a car being driven at high speed across rough ground.

The man holding Johnny let go and vanished into the fog. The other one thumped Bigmac hard in the stomach and followed him.

The car skidded to a halt and a fat vampire leapt out, shouting 'Make my night, make my night!'

Mr Atterbury unfolded himself a little more sedately from the driver's seat.

'It's all right, they're gone,' said Johnny. 'We'll never find them in this fog.'

There was the sound of an engine starting somewhere in the distance, and then wheels skidded out on to the unseen road.

'But I got the number!' shouted Wobbler, hopping from foot to foot. 'I dint have a pen so I huffed on the window and wrote it in the huff!'

'They were going to drive the bulldozer into the cemetery!' said Yo-less.

'Right in the huff, look!'

'Dear me, I expect a bit more than this of United Consolidated,' said Mr Atterbury. 'Hadn't we better see to your friend?'

Bigmac was kneeling on the ground, making small 'oof, oof' noises.

'I'll have to keep huffing on it to keep them there, mind!'

'You all right, Bigmac?'

They knelt down beside him. He was wheezing with his asthma.

'I . . . I really frightened him . . . yeah?' he managed.

'Right, right,' said Johnny. 'Come on, we'll give you a hand up . . .'

'I jus' saw them there—'

'How do you feel?'

'Jus' winded.'

'Hang on, I've got to go and huff on it again—'

'Help him into the car.'

''S'all right—'

'I'll drive him to the hospital, just in case.'

'No!'

Bigmac pushed them away, and rose unsteadily to his feet.

''m all right,' he said. 'Tough as old boots, me.'

Red and blue lights bloomed in the fog and a police siren *dee-dahed* once or twice and then stopped out of embarrassment.

'Ah,' said Mr Atterbury. 'I rather think my wife got a bit excited about things and phoned the police. Er . . . Bigmac, isn't it? Would you recognize those men if you saw them again?'

'Sure. One of 'em's got teethmarks in his ear.' Bigmac suddenly had the hunted look of one who has never quite seen eye to eye with the constabulary. 'But I ain't going in any police station. No way.'

Mr Atterbury straightened up as the police car crunched to a halt.

'I think it might be a good idea if I do most of the talking,' he said, when Sergeant Comely stepped out into the night. 'Ah, Ray,' he said. 'Glad you could drop by. Can I have a word?'

The boys stood in a huddle, watching as the men walked over to the bulldozer, and then inspected the remains of the wall.

'We're going to be in trouble,' said Bigmac. 'Old Comely's probably going to do me for ear-biting. Or pinching the bulldozer. You wait.'

Wobbler tapped Johnny on the shoulder.

'You *knew* something was going to happen,' he said.

'Yes. Don't know how.'

They watched the policemen peer into Mr Atterbury's car for a moment.

'He's reading my huff,' said Wobbler. 'That was lateral thinking, that was.'

Then Comely went back to the police car. They heard him speaking into the radio.

'No! I say again. That's H for Hirsute, W for Wagner – Wagner! Wagner! No! W as in Westphalia, A for Aardvark—'

Mr Atterbury appeared from the direction of the bulldozer, waving a pair of pliers.

'I don't think it's going to move again tonight,' he said.

'What's going to happen?' said Johnny.

'Not sure. We can probably trace the van. I think I've persuaded Sergeant Comely that we ought to deal with this quietly, for now. He'll take statements from you, though. That might be enough.'

'Were they from United Consolidated?'

The old man shrugged.

'Perhaps someone thought everything might be a lot simpler if the cemetery wasn't worth saving,' he said. 'Perhaps a couple of likely lads were slipped a handful of notes to do . . . er . . . a Halloween prank—'

There was a burst of noise from the police radio.

'We've stopped a van on the East Slate Road,' the sergeant called out. 'Sounds like our lads.'

'Well Done, Said PC Plonk,' said Yo-less, in a hollow voice. 'You Have Captured The Whole Gang! Good Work, Fumbling Four! And They All Went Home For Tea And Cakes.'

'It would help if you'd come along to the police station, Bigmac,' said Mr Atterbury.

'No way!'

'I'll come along with you. And one of your friends could come, too.'

'It'd really help,' said Johnny.

'I'll go with you,' said Yo-less.

'And then,' said Mr Atterbury, 'I'm going to take considerable pleasure in ringing up the chairman of United Consolidated. *Considerable* pleasure.'

It was ten minutes later. Bigmac had gone to the police station, accompanied by Yo-less and Mr Atterbury and an assurance that he wasn't going to be asked any questions about certain other minor matters relating to things like cars not being where the owners had expected them to be, and other things of that nature.

The sodium lights of Blackbury glowed in the fog, which was thinning out a bit now. They made the darkness beyond the carpet warehouse a lot deeper and much darker.

'Well, that's it, then,' said Wobbler. 'Game over. Let's go home.'

The fog was being torn apart by the wind. It was

even possible to see the moon through the flying streamers.

'Come on,' he repeated.

'It's still not right,' said Johnny. 'It can't end like this.'

'Best ending,' said Wobbler. 'Just like Yo-less said. Nasty men foiled. Kids save the day. Everyone gets a bun.'

The abandoned bulldozer seemed a lot bigger in this pale light.

The air had a fizz to it.

'Something's going to happen,' said Johnny, running towards the cemetery.

'Now, look—'

'Come on!'

'No! Not in there!'

Johnny turned around.

'And you're pretending to be a vampire?'

'But—'

'Come on, the railings have been knocked down.'

'But it's nearly midnight! And there's dead people in there!'

'Well? We're all dead, sooner or later.'

'Yeah, but *me*, I'd like it to be later, thank you!'

Johnny could feel it all around him – a squashed feel to things, like the air gets before a thunderstorm.

It cracked off the buckled gravestones and tingled on the dusty shrubberies.

The fog was pouring away now, as if it was trying to escape from something. The moon shone out of a damp blue-black sky casting darker shadows on the ground.

North Drive and East Way . . . they were still there, but they didn't look the same now. They belonged somewhere else – somewhere where people didn't take the roads of the dead and give them the names of the streets of the living . . .

'Wobbler?' said Johnny, without looking around.

'Yeah?'

'You there?'

'Yeah.'

'Thanks.'

He could feel something lifting off him, like a heavy blanket. He was amazed his feet still touched the ground.

He ran along North Drive, to the little area where all the dead roads met.

There was someone already there.

She spun around with her arms out and her eyes blissfully shut, the gravel crunching under her feet, the moonlight glinting off her ancient hat. All alone, twirling and twirling, Mrs Tachyon danced in the night.

Not all alone . . .

The air sparkled. Glowing lines, blue as electricity, thin as smoke, poured out of the clear sky. Where they touched the fingers of the dancing woman they stretched out and broke, then reformed.

They crawled over the grass. They whirred through the air. The whole cemetery was alive with pale blue comets.

Alive . . .

Mrs Tachyon's feet *were* off the ground.

Johnny looked at his own fingers. There was a blue glow crackling over his right hand, like St Elmo's Fire. It sparkled as he waved it towards the stars and felt his feet leave the gravel path.

'Ooowwwwwah!'

The lights spun him around and let him drift gently back down.

'Who *are* you?'

A line of fire screamed across the night and then exploded. Sparks flew out and traced lines in the air; which took on, as though it was outlined in neon, a familiar shape.

'Well, until tonight,' it said, blue fire sizzling in

215

his beard, 'I thought I was William Stickers. Watch this!'

Blue glows arched over the gravestones again and clustered around the dark bulk of the bulldozer, flowing across it so that it glowed.

The engine started.

There was a clash of gears.

It moved forward. The railings clanged and cartwheeled away. The brick wall crumbled.

Lights orbited around the bulldozer as it ploughed onward.

'Hey! Stop!'

Metal groaned. The engine note dropped to a dull, insistent throbbing.

The lights turned to look at Johnny. He could feel their attention.

'What are you *doing*?'

A light burst into a glittering diagram of the Alderman.

'Isn't this what people wanted?' he said. 'We don't need it any more. So if anyone's going to do it, it should be us. That's only right.'

'But you said this was your place!' said Johnny.

Mrs Sylvia Liberty outlined herself in the air.

'We have left Nothing there,' she said, 'of any Importance.'

'Force of habit,' said William Stickers, 'is what has subjugated the working man for too long. I was right about that, anyway.'

'The disgusting bolshevik, although he needs a shave, is Quite correct,' said Mrs Liberty. And then she laughed. 'It seems to me we've spent Far too long moping around because of what we're not, without any Consideration of what we might *be*.'

'Chronologically gifted,' said Mr Einstein, crackling into existence.

'Dimensionally advantaged,' said Mr Fletcher, sparkling like a flashbulb.

'Bodily unencumbered,' said the Alderman.

'Into Extra Time,' said Stanley Roundway.

'Enhanced,' said Mr Vicenti.

'We had to find it out,' said Mr Fletcher. 'You have to find it out. You have to forget who you were. That's the first step. And stop being frightened of old ghosts. Then you've got room to find out what you *are*. What you can *be*.'

'So we're off,' said the Alderman.

'Where to?'

'We don't know. It iss going to be very interesting to find out,' said Solomon Einstein.

'But . . . but . . . we've saved the cemetery!' said Johnny. 'We had a meeting! And Bigmac . . . and I spoke up and . . . there's been things on the television and people have really been *talking* about this place! No one's going to build anything on it! There's been birdwatchers here and everything! Turn the machine off! We've saved the cemetery.'

'But we don't need it any more,' said the Alderman.

'We do!'

The dead looked at him.

'We do,' Johnny repeated. 'We . . . need it to be there.'

The diesel engine chugged. The machine vibrated. The dead, if that's what they still were, seemed to be thinking.

Then Solomon Einstein nodded.

'This iss of course very true,' he said, in his excited squeaky voice. 'It all balances, you see. The living have to remember, the dead have to forget. Conservation of energy.'

The bulldozer's engine stuttered into silence.

Mr Vicenti held up a hand. It glowed like a firework.

'We came back to say goodbye. And thank you,' he said.

'I hardly did anything.'

'You listened. You tried. You were there. You can get medals just for being there. People forget the people who were just there.'

'Yes. I know.'

'But, now . . . we must be somewhere else.'

'No . . . don't go yet,' said Johnny. 'I have to ask you—'

Mr Vicenti turned.

'Yes?'

'Um . . .'

'Yes?'

'Are there . . . angels involved? You know? Or . . . devils and things? A lot of people would like to know.'

'Oh, no. I don't think so. That sort of thing . . . no. That's for the living. No.'

The Alderman rubbed his spectral hands. 'I rather think it's going to be a lot more interesting than that.'

The dead were walking away, some of them fading back into shining smoke as they moved.

Some were heading for the canal. There was a boat there. It looked vaguely like a gondola. A dark figure stood at one end, leaning on a pole that vanished into the water.

'This is my lift,' said William Stickers.

'It looks a bit . . . spooky. No offence meant,' said Johnny.

'Well, I thought I'd give it a try. If I don't like it, I'll go somewhere else,' said William Stickers, stepping aboard. 'Off we go, comrade.'

RIGHT said the ferryman.

The boat moved away from the bank. The canal was only a few metres wide, but the boat seemed to be drifting off a long, long way . . .

Voices came back over the waters.

'You know, an outboard motor on this and it'd go like a bird.'

I LIKE IT THE WAY IT IS, MR STICKERS.

'What's the pay like?'

SHOCKING.

'I wouldn't stand for it, if I was you—'

'I'm not sure where he's going,' said the Alderman, 'but he's certainly going to reorganize things when he gets there. Bit of a traditional thinker, our William.'

There was a click and hum from further along the bank. Einstein and Fletcher were sitting proudly in some sort of – well, it looked partly like an electronic circuit diagram, and partly like a machine, and partly like mathematics would look if it was solid. It glowed and fizzled.

'Good, isn't it,' said Mr Fletcher. 'You've heard of a train of thought?'

'This is a flight of the imagination,' said Solomon Einstein.

'We're going to have a good look at some things.'

'That's right. Starting with everything.'

Mr Fletcher thumped the machine happily.

'Right! The sky's the limit, Mr Einstein!'

'Not even that, Mr Fletcher!'

The lines grew bright, drew together, became more like a diagram. And vanished. Just before they vanished, though, they seemed to be accelerating.

And then there were three.

'Did I see them waving?' said Mrs Liberty.

'And particling, I shouldn't wonder,' said the Alderman. 'Come, Sylvia. I feel a more down-to-earth mode of transport would be suitable for us.'

He took her hand. They ignored Johnny and stepped on to the black waters of the canal.

And sank, slowly, leaving a pearly sheen on the water which gradually faded away.

Then there was the sound of a motor starting up.

Out of the water, transparent as a bubble, the

spirit of the dead Ford Capri rose gently towards the sky.

The Alderman wound down an invisible window.

'Mrs Liberty thinks we ought to tell you something,' he said. 'But . . . it's hard to explain, you know.'

'What is?' said Johnny.

'By the way, why are you wearing a pink sheet?'

'Um—'

'I expect it's not important.'

'Yes.'

'Well—' The car turned slowly; Johnny could see the moon through it. 'You know those games where this ball runs up and bounces around and ends up in a slot at the bottom?'

'Pinball machines?'

'Is that what they're called now?'

'I think so.'

'Oh. Right.' The Alderman nodded. 'Well . . . when you're bouncing around from pin to pin, it is probably very difficult to know that outside the game there's a room and outside the room there's a town and outside the town there's a country and outside the country there's a world and outside the world there's a billion trillion stars and that's only the start of it . . . but it's there, d'you see? Once you know about it, you can stop worrying about the slot at the bottom. And you might bounce around a good deal longer.'

'I'll . . . try to remember it.'

'Good man. Well, we'd better be going . . .'

Ghostly gears went crunch. The car juddered.

'Drat the thing. Ah . . . Be seeing you . . .'

It rose gently, turned towards the east, and sped away and up . . .

And then there was one.

'Well, I think I might as well be off,' said Mr Vicenti. He produced a top hat and an old-fashioned walking cane out of thin air.

'Why are you all leaving?' said Johnny.

'Oh, yes. It's Judgement Day,' said Mr Vicenti. 'We decided.'

'I thought that was chariots and things.'

'I think you'll have to use your own judgement on that one. No point in waiting for what you've already got. It's different for everybody, you see. Enjoy looking after the cemetery. They're places for the living, after all.'

Mr Vicenti pulled on a pair of white gloves and pressed an invisible lift button. He began to rise. White feathers cascaded out of his sleeves.

'Dear me,' he said, and opened his jacket. 'Go on, away with you! All of you! Shoo!'

Half a dozen ghostly pigeons untangled themselves and rocketed off into the dawn.

'There. That proves it. You can escape from anything, eventually,' he called down. Johnny just managed to hear him add, '. . . although I will admit that three sets of manacles, twenty feet of chain and a canvas sack can present a considerable amount of difficulty in certain circumstances . . .'

The light glinted off his hat.

And then there was . . . one.

Johnny turned around.

Mr Grimm was standing neatly in the middle of the path, with his neat hands neatly folded. Darkness surrounded him like a fog. He was watching the sky. Johnny had never seen such an expression . . .

He remembered the time, many years ago, when Bigmac had a party and hadn't invited him. He'd said afterwards, 'Well, of course not. I knew you'd come, you didn't have to be asked, you didn't need to be asked, you could just have turned up.' But everyone else was going to go, and was talking about going, and he'd felt like a pit had opened up in his life. That sort of thing was pretty awful when you were seven.

It looked much, much worse when you were dead.

Mr Grimm saw Johnny staring at him.

'Huh,' he said, pulling himself together. 'They'll be sorry.'

'I'm going to find out about you, Mr Grimm,' said Johnny.

'Nothing to find out,' snapped the ghost.

Johnny walked through him. There was a chilly moment, and then Mr Grimm was gone.

And then there were none.

Real night flowed back in. The sounds of the town, the distant hum of the traffic, filled the space taken up by the silence.

Johnny walked back along the gravel path.

'Wobbler?' he whispered. 'Wobbler?'

He found him crouched behind a gravestone with his eyes shut.

'Come on,' said Johnny.

'Look, I—'

'Everything's OK.'

'It was fireworks, right?' said Wobbler. His Count Dracula make-up was streaked and smudged, and he'd lost his fangs. 'Someone was letting some fireworks off, yes?'

'That's right.'

'Of course, I wasn't scared.'

'No.'

'But those things can be dangerous . . .'

'Oh, that's right.'

They turned as a rattling sound started up behind them. Mrs Tachyon appeared, pushing her shopping trolley; the wheels bounced and skidded on the gravel.

She ignored both of them. They stepped aside hurriedly as the trolley, one wheel squeaking, vanished into the gloom.

Then they walked home, through the morning mists.

Chapter 11

As Tommy Atkins had once said, things aren't necessarily over just because they've stopped.

There was Bigmac, for a start. Yo-less had gone home with him, and Bigmac's brother had been waiting up and had started on at him and Bigmac had looked at him strangely for a few seconds and then hit him so hard that he knocked him out. Yo-less said, with awe in his voice, that it'd been so hard that the word 'TAH' was printed in Biro on the brother's chin. And then he'd growled at Clint and the dog had hid under the sofa. So Yo-less had to get his mother out of bed to bring her car round to carry Bigmac's suitcase, three tropical fish tanks and two hundred copies of *Guns and Ammo* back to her spare room.

And there was the generous donation to the

Blackbury Volunteers by United Amalagamated
Consolidated Holdings. As Mr Atterbury said, it's
amazing what you can do with a kind word, pro-
vided you've also got a big stick.

The cemetery was already looking more lived-in.
There were endless arguments between the
Volunteers who wanted it to be habitat and the
ones who wanted it to be ecology and a middle
group who just wanted it to be clean and tidy, but
at least it was wanted, which seemed to Johnny to
be the most important thing.

It took Johnny a week to find what he wanted,
and when he found it he took it along to the cemetery after school, when no one was about. There
was frost on the ground.

'Mr Grimm?'

He found him by the canal, sitting staring at the
water.

'Mr Grimm?'

'Go away. You're dangerous.'

'I thought you'd be a bit . . . lonely. So I bought
you this.'

He opened the bag.

'Mr Atterbury helped,' he said. 'He phoned
around some of his friends who've got electrical
shops. It's been repaired. It'll work until the

batteries die, and then I thought maybe it'd work on ghost batteries.'

'What is it?'

'A very small television,' said Johnny. 'I thought I could put it right in a bush or somewhere and no one'll know it's there except you.'

'What are you doing this for?' said Mr Grimm, suspiciously.

'Because I looked you up in the newspaper. May the twenty-first, nineteen twenty-seven. There wasn't very much. Just the bit about them finding . . . you in the canal, and the coroner's inquest.'

'Oh? Poking around, eh? And what do you think you know about *anything*?'

'Nothing.'

'I don't have to explain.'

'Is that why you couldn't leave with the others?'

'What? I can leave whenever I like,' said the ghost of Mr Grimm, very quickly. 'If I'm staying here, it's because I want to be here. I know my place. I know how to do the right thing. I could leave whenever I want. But I've got more pride than that. People like you don't understand that. You don't take life seriously.'

It hadn't been a long report in the paper. Mr Vicenti was right. In those days, some things didn't get a lot of reporting. Mr Grimm had been a respectable citizen, keeping his head down, a man at the back of the crowd, and then his business had failed and there'd been some other trouble involving money, and then there'd been the canal. Mr Grimm had taken life very seriously, starting with his own.

People didn't talk much about that sort of thing in those days. Suicide was against the law. Johnny had wondered why. It meant that if you missed, or the gas ran out, or the rope broke, you could get locked up in prison to show you that life was really very jolly and thoroughly worth living.

Mr Grimm sat with his hands clasped around his knees.

Johnny realized that he could think of nothing to say, so he said nothing.

Instead, he wedged the little pocket television deep in a bush, where no one, not even the keenest birdwatcher, would find it.

'Can you turn it on with your mind?' he said.

'Who says I shall want to?'

The picture came on, and there was the faint tinkly sound of the familiar signature tune.

'Let's see,' said Johnny. 'You've missed a

week . . . Mrs Swede has just found out Janine didn't go to the party . . . Mr Hatt has sacked Jason from the shop because he thinks he took the money . . . and . . .'

'I see.'

'So . . . I'll be off, then, shall I?'

'Right.'

Johnny backed away.

'I'm sure the hours'll just fly by.'

'Right.'

'So . . . cheerio, then.'

'Right.'

'Mr Grimm?' Johnny wanted to say: you can leave any time you want. But there seemed to be no point.

'Right.'

Johnny watched for a while, and then turned and walked away. The other three were waiting for him by the phone box.

'Was he there?' said Yo-less.

'Yes.'

'What's he doing now?'

'Watching television,' said Johnny.

'I expect ghosts do that a lot,' said Wobbler.

''Spect so.'

'You all right?'

'Just thinking about the difference between heaven and hell.'

'That doesn't sound like "all right" to me.'

Johnny blinked. And looked around at the world. It was, not to put too fine a point on it, wonderful. Which wasn't the same as nice. It wasn't even the same as good. But it was full of . . . stuff. You'd never get to the end of it. It was always springing new things on you . . .

'Yeah,' he said. 'All right. What shall we do now?'

ABOUT THE AUTHOR

TERRY PRATCHETT is one of the most popular authors writing today. He is particularly well known for the phenomenally successful Discworld series, which includes three titles for younger readers – *The Amazing Maurice and his Educated Rodents*, *The Wee Free Men* and *A Hat Full of Sky*.

Terry's books have appeared on a number of children's award shortlists, and *The Amazing Maurice and his Educated Rodents* won the 2001 Carnegie Medal.

Terry Pratchett lives in Wiltshire, and finds his days are rather full.

JOHNNY AND THE BOMB
Terry Pratchett

It's May 21, 1941, thought Johnny. It's war.

Johnny Maxwell and his friends have to do *something* when they find Mrs Tachyon, the local bag lady, semi-conscious in an alley . . . as long as it's not the kiss of life.

But there's more to Mrs Tachyon than a squeaky trolley and a bunch of dubious black bags. Somehow she holds the key to different times, different eras – including the Blackbury Blitz in 1941. Suddenly *now* isn't the safe place Johnny once thought it was, as he finds himself caught up more and more with *then* . . .

SMARTIES PRIZE, SILVER MEDAL WINNER SHORTLISTED FOR THE CARNEGIE MEDAL and THE CHILDREN'S BOOK AWARD.

'Enormously entertaining and contains more wry observations than you could shake a Heinkel at' *Daily Telegraph*

From the author of the phenomenally successful *Discworld®* series and *The Amazing Maurice and His Educated Rodents*, which won the 2001 Carnegie Medal.

ISBN 0 552 551 04 X

**ONLY YOU CAN
SAVE MANKIND**
Terry Pratchett

IF NOT YOU, WHO ELSE?

As the mighty alien fleet from the latest computer game thunders across the screen, Johnny prepares to blow them into the usual million pieces. And they send him a message: *We surrender*.

They're not supposed to do that! They're supposed to die. And computer joysticks don't have 'Don't Fire' buttons . . .

SHORTLISTED FOR THE GUARDIAN CHILDREN'S FIC-TION AWARD

'An impressively original book with its thrills and spills, its inventiveness, its wit and continuous readability' *Daily Telegraph*

From the author of the phenomenally successful *Discworld®* series and *The Amazing Maurice and His Educated Rodents*, which won the 2001 Carnegie Medal.

ISBN 0 552 55103 1

THE WEE FREE MEN
Terry Pratchett

'Crivens! Whut aboot us, ye daftie!'

There's trouble on the Aching farm – nightmares spreading down from the hills. And Tiffany Aching's little brother has been stolen away. To get him back, Tiffany has a weapon (a frying pan), her granny's magic book (well, *Diseases of the Sheep*) – and the Nac Mac Feegle, the Wee Free Men, the fightin', thievin', tiny blue-skinned pictsies who were thrown out of Fairyland for being Drunk and Disorderly . . .

Set on the Discworld®, this wise, witty and wonderfully inventive adventure comes from the author of *The Amazing Maurice and His Educated Rodents*, winner of the 2001 Carnegie Medal.

'Quite, quite brilliant' *Starburst*

'Plenty to laugh at here, not least Pratchett's ability to put a 90 degree spin on the familiar' *The Times*

'A clear example of a comic fantasy classic and well . . . Crivens! It deserves t'sell a millyun copies' *Sunday Express*

ISBN 0 552 54905 3

THE AMAZING MAURICE
AND HIS EDUCATED RODENTS
Terry Pratchett

Maurice, a streetwise tomcat, has the perfect money-making scam. *Everyone* knows the stories about rats and pipers, and Maurice has a stupid-looking kid with a pipe, and his very own plague of rats – strangely *educated* rats . . .

But in Bad Blintz, the little con suddenly goes down the drain. For someone there is playing a *different* tune and now the rats must learn a new word.

EVIL.

It's not a game any more. It's a rat-eat-rat world. And that might only be the start . . .

'Ethically challenging, beautifully orchestrated, philosophically opposed to the usual plot fixes of fantasy' *Guardian*

'Simply gripping story-telling' *The Times*

ISBN 0 552 54693 3

THE CARPET PEOPLE
Terry Pratchett

In the beginning, there was nothing but endless flatness. Then came the Carpet . . .

That's the old story everyone knows and loves (even if they don't really believe it).

But now the Carpet is home to many different tribes and peoples and there's a new story in the making. The story of Fray, sweeping a trail of destruction across the Carpet. The story of power-hungry mouls – and of two Munrung brothers, who set out on an adventure to end all adventures when their village is flattened.

It's a story that will come to a terrible end – if someone doesn't do something about it. If everyone doesn't do something about it . . .

A hilarious fantasy, co-written by Terry Pratchett, aged seventeen, and master storyteller, Terry Pratchett, aged forty-three.

'Only a writer with a masterstroke of imagination could place an entire empire of goodies and baddies within the fronds of a carpet' *Daily Mail*

From the author of *The Amazing Maurice and His Educated Rodents*, winner of the Carnegie Medal.

ISBN 0 552 55105 8

THE BROMELIAD
Terry Pratchett

Truckers
To the thousands of tiny nomes living under the floorboards of a large department store, there is no Outside. No Day or Night, no Sun or Rain. They're just daft old legends. Until the devastating news that the Store is to be demolished. Now the nomes have to think. And they have to think BIG . . .

ISBN 0 552 55100 7

Diggers
A Bright New Dawn is just around the corner for the nomes when they move into an abandoned quarry. Or is it? For when humans turn up, they begin to mess everything up again. Now the nomes have two choices: to run, or to hide. Or, maybe, they could . . . *fight*. But for how long can they keep the humans at bay – even with the help of the monster Jekub?

ISBN 0 552 55101 5

Wings
It's a ridiculous plan. Impossible. To hitch a ride on a truck with wings – Concorde. And then steal one of those space shuttle things. But home is home, and the nomes want to get there. They don't *mean* to cause any trouble. Really . . .

ISBN 0 552 55102 3

Hilariously inventive, marvellously witty and highly original, *Truckers*, *Diggers* and *Wings* form a magnificent trilogy of tales about a race of little people struggling to survive in a world full of humans: *The Bromeliad Trilog*y.